Charm Hall
The Magic Begins

Tabitha Black

Hodder
Children's
Books

A division of Hachette Children's Books

Special thanks to Narinder Dhami

1

A Catalogue record for this book is available from the British Library

ISBN 978 0 340 93140 0

Typeset in Weiss by Avon DataSet Ltd,
Bidford on Avon, Warwickshire

Printed and bound in Great Britain by
Clays Ltd, St Ives plc

The paper and board used in this paperback by Hodder Children's
Books are natural recyclable products made from wood grown in
sustainable forests. The manufacturing processes conform to the
environmental regulations of the country of origin.

Hodder Children's Books
a division of Hachette Children's Books
338 Euston Road, London NW1 3BH
An Hachette Livre UK company

Chapter One

"I am *not* nervous," Paige Hart said firmly to herself. "And I don't feel sick. I'm *fine*." She took a deep breath to clear her thoughts and calm her nerves.

Everything had happened so fast. One minute she was getting ready to go back to Oaklands School and see all her friends after the Easter break. The next minute her life had been turned upside down and now here she was, standing outside the headteacher's office at Charm Hall Boarding School for Girls.

Her father, an engineer, had suddenly been sent to Dubai by his company, and Paige's mum had gone with him. They would be away for a year, and so Paige was here at boarding school. She felt nervous and excited all at the same time. Nervous because the school year was already two terms in, which meant everyone else would have already made friends by now. And excited because Charm Hall was a big old mansion house set in beautiful grounds and Paige thought living here could turn out to be a lot of fun.

Just then, footsteps coming down the corridor behind her made Paige jump. A tall girl with a cheerful face and blonde hair in a bob was coming towards her. Paige thought she'd pass by without saying a word, but she didn't. She stopped and stared at Paige curiously.

"Are you OK?" the girl asked with a frown. "You look like you're about to throw up!"

Paige didn't quite know what to say. *No, I'm not* wouldn't really be true, and *Yes, I am!* sounded a bit gross.

"I felt just the same on my first day back in September," the girl continued without waiting for Paige's response. "I'm Shannon Carroll. Nice to meet you."

Paige smiled at her. She liked the look of this girl. "Thanks. I'm Paige Hart."

Shannon's face split into a smile and she was just about to say something else when the door of the office opened and Miss Linnet came out. Paige had already met the headmistress briefly when her parents had brought her to look round the school.

"Paige, my dear, I'm sorry to have kept you waiting," she said. "Do come in." Her kindly cornflower-blue eyes, framed by silver-rimmed glasses, flicked to Shannon Carroll. "And, Shannon, I'm glad you're here. Would you mind waiting for a few moments while I speak to Paige?"

"Of course not, Miss Linnet," Shannon said.

Paige followed the headmistress's tall, slim figure into the office, glancing back at Shannon over her shoulder. Shannon gave Paige a thumbs-up sign and mouthed, "See you later!" Paige smiled to herself. She hoped she would be in the same class as Shannon.

Miss Linnet's office was large and airy, with sunlight streaming through the tall, pointed windows. The walls were lined with bookshelves, and a vase of pink lilies stood on the wooden desk.

Paige looked round curiously. Behind Miss Linnet's chair hung a large portrait in an ornate gold frame. It showed a woman in a purple gown with a black kitten sitting on her lap.

"That's Lavinia Charm, the founder of our school," Miss Linnet said, seeing that Paige was looking at the picture. "It's almost one hundred years since the school was founded. Do sit down." She moved over to her desk and sat down herself. "Now I know this must all seem very sudden and rather scary for you," she said, smiling warmly at Paige, "but I'm sure you're going to love Charm Hall. It can be a lot of fun with three hundred and fifty girls around!"

Paige could hear pride and affection in the headmistress's voice, and she felt excited. After all, a year wasn't for ever. She could email and phone her mum and dad, and visit them during the holidays. And it would be fun living with lots of other girls.

"We have four houses: Hummingbird, Nightingale, Swan and Peacock," Miss Linnet explained, "and each student belongs to one of them. You'll be in Hummingbird."

Paige nodded, wondering which house Shannon belonged to.

"As you already know, you'll be joining Miss Mackenzie's form," Miss Linnet went on. "And you'll be sharing a dorm with two other girls who are in your class: Summer Kirby and Shannon Carroll."

Paige's face lit up. "Cool!" she said.

"I'm glad you approve!" Miss Linnet laughed. "And now I'm going to ask Shannon to take you to your dorm. I know that your new roommates have been looking forward to your arrival. But first . . ." she stood up, came round the desk to Paige, and held out her hand, ". . . let me officially welcome you to Charm Hall. I hope you're going to be very happy here."

Shyly Paige shook the headmistress's hand. Then Miss Linnet headed over to the door. As she did so, Paige found her gaze immediately sliding back to the portrait of Lavinia Charm. Somehow, her eyes seemed drawn to the little black kitten. She just couldn't take her eyes off it. There was something about the way the kitten looked out of the painting at her that made Paige feel tingly with excitement. And then, suddenly, as she stared at the picture, the kitten blinked!

Paige felt her jaw drop. She stared at the kitten, waiting for it to move again, but nothing happened. Paige blinked herself and shook her head. *I must have imagined it*, she thought.

The sound of Miss Linnet opening the door made her turn away from the picture, in time to see Shannon, who was leaning against the wood-panelled wall outside, spring to attention.

"Shannon, I want you to take Paige to your dorm," Miss Linnet said. "I'm putting you in charge of showing her round and helping her settle in."

"Cool!" Shannon exclaimed, then looked puzzled when Paige and Miss Linnet both smiled. "This way."

The headmistress disappeared back into her office and shut the door, while Paige hurried after Shannon.

"I'm glad you're in our room," Shannon went on. "It's just been me and Summer since we started in September. We've been looking forward to having a new roommate."

Paige opened her mouth to ask what Summer was like, but Shannon didn't give her a chance.

"I guess I should give you the lowdown about the school. It's pretty special," she said. "It used to be a proper manor house. That's why there are all these massive rooms and high ceilings and old oak staircases."

Shannon was whisking Paige along corridor after corridor as she talked. Along the way Paige managed to peep into a few of the empty classrooms. The wood-panelled rooms were enormous, with high, carved ceilings and tall Gothic windows.

"This is really different from my old school," Paige remarked as they went down yet another passageway. "Oaklands was really modern."

"Oh, Charm's great for playing hide-and-seek," Shannon replied with a grin. "There are all sorts of interesting hiding places. Like this . . ." She stepped forward and pulled open a door underneath the staircase they were passing. Paige hadn't even noticed the door, as it was made of the same wood as the surrounding panels. She peeped in and saw a small triangular-shaped room, packed with music stands and sheet music.

"There's the gym," Shannon said, closing the

cupboard door and pointing down the passage. Through the open door Paige could see ropes and wall bars. "And around the corner is the dining hall. The food's actually quite good. Anyway, we're allowed to have food parcels from home, and Summer's dad makes the best cakes! Oh, and this is the art studio."

Paige peered round the door of the art studio as Shannon took off down the corridor again. The studio was light and airy, and there were a couple of older girls in the corner bent over a potter's wheel. Paige had never tried pottery before but it looked fun. All of a sudden, Paige saw a flash of black fur and the tip of a tail slipping under a desk. There was a cat in the studio! Paige tried to see where it was going, but it had disappeared from sight.

"It's so cool that Charm Hall has its own cat," Paige said as she caught up with Shannon again.

"No. No cat," Shannon said, looking at Paige strangely. "There are no pets allowed in school."

"Oh, I see," Paige replied, feeling rather stupid. "It's just that I could have sworn I just saw a cat in the art studio."

"Your eyes must be playing tricks on you,"

Shannon said, grinning. "You should talk to Summer about it. Her mum's an optician, maybe she could help," she joked. Then she raced on again over to the window.

"Now, if you look out of that window, you can see the netball and tennis courts and the hockey field at the back of the school," she went on as Paige hurried after her. "Our dorm's at the top of the house on the third floor." She paused at the bottom of a wide staircase, her hand on the wooden banister, and waited for Paige to catch up. "Sorry! I'm going on a bit, aren't I? I do sometimes. Feel free to tell me to shut up!"

"Oh, I was just going to buy a pair of earplugs," Paige replied, straight-faced.

Shannon stared at her for a second and then the two of them burst out laughing.

"I don't *want* you to shut up!" Paige grinned. "I love hearing about Charm Hall."

"Well, is there anything you want to ask me?" Shannon went on.

Paige shook her head. "At the moment I'm just wondering how I'm ever going to find my way around!" she admitted.

"You will," Shannon said confidently. "After you've unpacked, Summer and I will take you round the grounds."

"By the way, which house are you in?" asked Paige, remembering what Miss Linnet had said.

"Hummingbird," Shannon replied, leading Paige up a tall, winding, wooden staircase. "And so is Summer."

"So am I," Paige announced happily. "What's Summer like?" she added curiously.

"Oh, she's great," Shannon replied. "She's the youngest in our year, brilliant at gymnastics and, you'll be glad to know, she doesn't talk half as much as I do!"

Shannon was running up the stairs, two at a time. Paige was a little slower because she was staring at the banisters. She'd noticed that there were tiny mice carved into the wood here and there. They were running up and down the banisters, tails flying. And when Paige looked more closely, she noticed that there was a little carved kitten peeping playfully out at the mice from behind a knot in the wood. It reminded her of the kitten in the portrait. *How sweet*, Paige thought, but her thoughts were interrupted as a girl came round a curve in the stairs towards them and almost bumped into Shannon.

The girl frowned, putting her hands on her hips. She had long blonde hair and a pretty but sharp-featured face.

"You nearly knocked me over, Shannon Carroll!" she said accusingly. "You know you're not supposed to run on the stairs." She threw Paige a disdainful look. "And who's the newbie, anyway?"

"Paige Hart, meet Abigail Carter," Shannon said coolly.

Abigail looked Paige up and down as if she was something the cat had dragged in. Then she turned to Shannon. "Well, if she's already made friends with *you*, I think that tells me everything I need to know about her," Abigail said rudely. She glanced back at Paige. "A little word of advice, newbie. If you want to fit in at Charm Hall, don't listen to *anything* Shannon tells you!"

Then she flounced past Paige and Shannon and hurried down the stairs without another word.

Chapter Two

Paige stared after Abigail, hardly able to believe her ears. "What a welcome!" she said.

"That's Abigail for you," Shannon sighed. Then she winked at Paige. "You can see how much she likes me!"

"Please tell me she's not in our class," Paige said, pulling a face as they began to climb to the second storey.

"Do you want the bad news or the bad news?" Shannon asked, grinning. "Abigail's pushy, nosy and a total pain in the neck. And those are her good points. Just ignore her. Summer and I do!"

"I'll try," Paige said, laughing, "but something tells me that Abigail isn't an easy person to ignore."

The stairs were getting steeper and more winding now.

"Is it much further?" Paige panted, stopping to catch her breath. She leaned against the wall and felt something knobbly behind her. Paige glanced round to see a stone gargoyle with bulging eyes, big ears and large fangs glaring back at her.

"Meet our gargoyle," Shannon said. "Summer and I always pat him on the head for luck when we go by."

"He's pretty ugly," Paige remarked, assessing the stone figure. "But cute in his own special way!"

"Paige, you're a girl after my own heart," Shannon said, patting the gargoyle's head affectionately.

They went on up the stairs.

"We're almost there," Shannon said encouragingly. "We're in Lilac Dorm, which used to be one of the attics. The biggest dorms have six girls, but three is really cosy." She flung open the door nearest to the top of the stairs. "Big drum roll. Ta-da! Here we are!"

Paige hurried up the last few creaking steps, dying to get her first glimpse of the room which would be her new home. "Oh, it's great!" she cried, taking in the airy, sunny space with its sloping ceilings, cupboards slotted under the eaves and two gabled windows. Her trunk had already been brought up and left at the end of one of the beds, which stood under a window and was covered with a patchwork quilt. A desk and chair stood next to the bed.

There were two other beds in the room, and on one of them sat a shy-looking girl with long dark hair and quite amazingly blue eyes. She put down the book she was reading and smiled at Paige.

"Summer, this is Paige Hart, our new roommate," Shannon explained. "Now don't go chattering on and on and wear her out. I've warned you about that before!"

Summer laughed, and Paige guessed that Shannon was teasing her because she looked a bit quiet.

"Hello, Paige," Summer said, her voice soft but friendly. "I hope you're going to like it here."

"Thanks," Paige replied as she wandered over to

the window. The view from the attic was spectacular. Below her were the green lawns that surrounded the school, studded with ancient spreading oak trees, towering cedars and rhododendron bushes covered in lilac and crimson flowers. Beyond the lawns the shrubs and trees grew more closely together until they gradually merged into woodland.

Paige turned back to the others. "You know, I think I *am* going to like it here," she said smiling.

"Of course you are!" Shannon declared. "How

could you not, with two fantastic roommates like Summer and me?" She opened one of the cupboards to reveal a rail and shelves inside. "This is your wardrobe, Paige."

Paige unlocked her trunk. Meanwhile, Shannon flung herself down on her bed and carried on talking.

"This term's going to be great!" she said happily, "Unfortunately you've already missed sports day, that was last term, but there's loads of stuff going on: trips and picnics and concerts. Oh, yes, and in a few days' time Lavinia Charm's birthday is coming up. Apparently the school always has a special party on that day, and a big birthday cake."

"Oh, yes, Lavinia Charm," Paige said thoughtfully. "I saw her portrait in Miss Linnet's office."

Shannon nodded. "It'll be Founder's Day too, in a few weeks' time," she said with a grin. "Charm Hall School will be exactly one hundred years old."

As Paige began to unpack her trunk, Summer came over to help her and began scooping the clothes up and putting them neatly in the cupboard. Paige smiled. Shannon and Summer seemed very different, but she liked them both already.

"What about the teachers?" Paige asked curiously.

"Well, Miss Linnet's *really* cool, of course," Shannon said, plumping up her pillows and lying down again. "So is Miss Drake. She's one of the games teachers."

"Watch out for Mrs Stark the maths teacher," Summer chipped in, helping Paige to hang up her school shirts. "Nobody likes her much. But most of the teachers are really nice, like Miss Collins, who teaches English, and Mrs Bloomfield, the dorm-mother, who oversees all our rooms."

"Yes, she's lovely, especially if you're ill," Shannon added. "She can be quite strict, though. Hey!" She sat bolt upright on her bed. "I know what we'll do: we'll have a midnight feast to welcome Paige to Charm Hall!"

"A midnight feast?" Paige was excited. With no brothers and sisters of her own, midnight feasts were not something she was used to.

Summer nodded. "Whenever we get a food parcel from home, Shannon and I have a midnight feast," she explained.

"Don't the teachers mind?" asked Paige.

"Well, of *course* they do!" Shannon laughed. "We're not allowed to lock our dorm doors and it's lights out at nine. So when we're having a midnight feast, we have to be extra quiet in case Mrs Bloomfield comes in and catches us. It all adds to the fun!"

Paige grinned. "You know I said I thought I was going to like it here?"

Summer and Shannon nodded.

"Well, forget that," Paige laughed. "I think I'm going to *love* it here!"

Chapter Three

Paige curled further into the window seat and kept as still and as quiet as she could. She was in one of the busiest of the school corridors and she could hear footsteps passing to and fro. But the thick, green velvet curtains pulled across the window seat meant that nobody knew she was there. It was Saturday and the day of Lavinia Charm's birthday. Later that afternoon there would be the school party to celebrate, but for now Paige was playing hide-and-seek with her new friends.

Paige looked at the stained-glass panels in the window. The glass was brilliantly coloured and each small pane depicted a different animal. One had a white unicorn with a silver horn, another a golden phoenix rising from orange and crimson flames. There was a dragon with brilliant red and green scales, a mysterious-looking Sphinx, and even a black kitten.

That kitten gets everywhere! Paige thought, tracing her finger over the outline of the cat. Even now, a week after she'd arrived at Charm Hall, she was still noticing unusual little details around the school. It was part of what made Charm Hall so different.

"Got you!"

The curtains were swept aside by Shannon, who stood there grinning at Paige. "I thought I was *never* going to find you!" she laughed. "I've caught everyone else!"

She was joined by Summer, along with Penny Harris and Grace Wilson. The girls were all in the same form group, and Paige had got to know them quite well over the last few days. Although Shannon, Paige and Summer were still nine, Penny and Grace had already turned ten. None of them were too old for hide-and-seek, though, especially not when there were so many great places to hide.

"How did you find me?" Paige asked, scrambling off the window seat.

Shannon lifted a strand of Paige's long auburn hair. "I could see a bit of your hair poking out from behind the curtain," she explained. "I'd know that colour anywhere!"

"Have we got time for another game?" asked Paige.

Penny shook her head. "We'd better go and tidy our dorm," she said to Grace. "We'll get into trouble with Mrs Bloomfield if we don't. It looks like a hurricane's hit it!"

"How about a game of tennis before we get ready for the party?" Shannon suggested to Paige and Summer as the other girls hurried off.

"Actually, I want to email my mum and dad," Paige replied. "Why don't you and Summer go? I'll see you back in the dorm."

Shannon and Summer went to get their tennis kit, and Paige hurried off to the computer room. Miss Linnet had told her she could email her mum and dad whenever she liked for the first few months while she was settling in. Paige was pleased because it meant she could use the computer room outside of the set times, when it was a bit quieter. She'd sent a very short email the day after she arrived, just to let her parents know she was OK, but now she had lots to tell them about her first few days at Charm.

Dear Mum and Dad,

It's really warm and sunny today, but I bet it's much warmer in Dubai! Has Dad's sunburn gone yet?

I didn't have time to tell you much about Shannon and Summer in my last email, but we're really good friends now. Shannon talks a lot and likes to be the leader, but Summer and I don't mind because she's really fun and always has brilliant ideas. It was her idea to have a midnight feast to welcome me to the school, and we sat up late eating doughnuts and crisps! It was great.

Summer is much quieter but sometimes she comes out with the funniest things. She's amazing at gymnastics and can even do the splits. Abigail Carter tried to copy her in the gym the other day, and almost split her shorts! Abigail's in our class. She's very brainy, but she always wants to be best at everything. On Wednesday, in English, she got really annoyed because Shannon got an A for her short story and Abigail only got an A-. She looked so mad, I thought that steam was going to come out of her ears!

There are about seventy girls in our year, but only twenty-five in our class. Our form teacher, Miss Mackenzie, is quite young and very nice, but she can be strict too. And everyone loves Miss Linnet, even though you kind of get the feeling that she knows just what you're thinking when she looks at you.

Today is Lavinia Charm's birthday, and we're having a party! She's the founder of the school.

Paige glanced up at the clock. Although it was Saturday and the girls didn't have to study, she wanted to spend some time working on *A Midsummer Night's Dream* before the party. The others had been studying the play in their English class since the previous term, and Paige felt that she had some catching-up to do. She decided to finish her email and head up to the dorm.

Please don't worry about me, because I'm having a great time! she typed. I love it here. Hope to hear from you soon. Love, Paige.

Paige added a row of kisses and clicked the Send button. She waited until the email had gone and then closed down the computer. Quickly she hurried out into the corridor and bumped straight into Abigail Carter.

"Look where you're going, can't you?" Abigail snapped, but almost immediately a look of spiteful

glee spread across her face. "What were you doing in the computer room anyway?"

"If it's any of your business, I was emailing my mum and dad," Paige said shortly, heading off down the corridor.

"We're not allowed to use the computer room outside of the set times," Abigail called out smugly. "I shall have to tell the teacher on duty that I saw you coming out of there!"

Paige spun round to face her. "OK. I'll come with you," she said calmly.

"What?" Abigail looked stunned.

"I'll come with you," Paige repeated. "And explain that Miss Linnet gave me permission to email my mum and dad whenever I like for the first month or two." She smiled sweetly at Abigail. "Let's go, shall we?"

Frowning crossly, Abigail whirled round and stomped away.

Paige shook her head. *What is her problem?* she thought as she made her way up to the dorm. Abigail was pretty and clever, as well as being good at games, but she always seemed to want to get the better of everyone else, just to make herself feel better. Paige couldn't understand it.

The attic dorm was empty. It was also stiflingly hot, so Paige went over to the windows and flung them open. Below her, she could see girls starting to stream into the school to get ready for the party, but Paige guessed that Shannon and Summer would play on till the last minute before rushing inside. They both loved tennis.

She sat down at her desk and reached for *A Midsummer Night's Dream*. Paige had never read any Shakespeare before and she found the language quite difficult, but the story was magical. It was all about fairies and people getting lost in the woods and having spells cast on them.

Paige was soon so caught up in the play that she didn't notice the sunshine fade to be replaced by a gloomy grey light. Suddenly, large raindrops began to patter in through the open windows, soaking into the curtains. Paige frowned. "What happened to the sun?" she murmured.

The window on the other side of the room had come free of its latch. As the wind picked up, it banged to and fro, making a terrible din. Paige got up and ran over to close it. Looking out, she could see girls running into the school from all directions as the rain pelted down. A flash of silver lightning lit up the sky and as the rumble of thunder filled the room Paige went to close the window near her bed.

But just as she was reaching up to pull the window shut, she heard a tiny sound. It was almost like a – Paige shook her head – no, it *couldn't* be.

Miaow!

But there it was again. And then, suddenly, a tiny, wet black kitten jumped on to the window sill. It stared inquisitively at Paige with large, almond-shaped golden eyes, and then leaped lightly down on to her bed and curled up on the patchwork quilt.

Chapter Four

Paige couldn't believe what she was seeing. She stared at the kitten in amazement. "Hello, sweetie!" she said gently, sitting down on the bed beside her. "Where did *you* come from?"

The kitten gave a little chirrup and immediately climbed trustingly on to Paige's lap. Her fur was so wet it stuck up in tiny spikes.

"Oh, you're all wet!" Paige exclaimed. "Let's get something to dry you off."

Carrying the cat, Paige found an old sweatshirt in her wardrobe. She wrapped the kitten up in it with just her furry face poking out, and gently rubbed her dry. The kitten didn't seem to mind at all. She began to purr loudly like a tiny rumbling engine. Outside the storm raged on, the thunder becoming louder and the lightning flashes more frequent.

"Hi, Paige," Summer said, shaking back her damp fringe as she entered the room, tennis racquet in hand. "Shannon didn't want to come in until we'd finished the game, but the rain got so bad that we couldn't carry on. She's just gone to return the tennis balls to—" She stopped short, staring at the bundle in Paige's arms. Paige couldn't help laughing at the stunned look on her friend's face.

"A kitten!" Summer cried incredulously. "Where did it come from?"

"Through the window," Paige replied. "She was soaked, but I think she's dried off a bit now." She unwrapped the kitten and put her on the bed so that Summer could see. The kitten sat down and began to wash herself busily with her pink tongue, smoothing down her ruffled fur. Paige and Summer watched, smiling.

"Oh, she's gorgeous!" Summer breathed. She held out her hand to the kitten who immediately lost interest in grooming herself and began headbutting Summer's fingers gently. "Look at her collar. Isn't it unusual?"

Paige had been too concerned with drying the kitten to take much notice before, but now she took a closer look. The collar was made of velvet and was a purplish-red colour, exactly the shade of a ripe plum.

"Yes, I've never seen one like it before," she said.

The kitten had rolled over now and was inviting them to tickle her tummy.

"I love cats," Summer told Paige. "We've got a tabby at home called Mopsy."

Just then the door opened again.

"We'll have to finish the game tomorrow, Summer," Shannon said, bustling into the room, a towel around her neck. "I'm soaked and—" Like Summer, Shannon broke off and came to a dead halt when she saw the kitten. Her mouth dropped wide open. Paige and Summer laughed.

"Is that a *kitten*?" Shannon spluttered.

"Got it in one, Shannon!" Paige replied.

"Isn't she cute?" said Summer. She had found a hair ribbon and was dangling it above the kitten's

head. The kitten batted at it playfully and tried to
catch it with her tiny claws.

"But pets aren't allowed in school!" Shannon
pointed out. "Where did it come from?"

"We do see cats around the school grounds
sometimes," Summer pointed out.

"Yes, around the *grounds*!" Shannon exclaimed.
"Not inside the school. And they're usually fully
grown cats, not kittens. How did it get in?"

"She jumped through the window on to my bed,"
explained Paige.

"And we can't possibly put her back outside in the middle of a storm!" Summer added firmly, as another loud thunderclap echoed round the room.

Shannon went and peered out of the window next to Paige's bed. "But how did she get up on to the roof in the first place?" she asked. "It looks much too far for a kitten to climb!"

"I suppose she must have got into the school somehow, and then climbed out of an open window on to the roof," Summer suggested.

Meanwhile, the kitten padded across the patchwork quilt towards Shannon and tapped her knee gently with one furry paw, mewing loudly. Shannon smiled and sat down on the bed to stroke the kitten's damp fur.

"She *is* cute, isn't she?" she said. Paige and Summer both nodded. "Oh, well, I suppose she'll have to stay for a bit!" Shannon went on, tickling the kitten under her chin. "At least until the storm's over anyway. And if she's going to be here for a while, we'd better give her a name."

"How about 'Velvet'?" suggested Summer. "Because of her collar."

"Good idea," Paige agreed.

Shannon nodded. "Velvet, welcome to Charm Hall!" she said smiling.

The kitten looked round at the three girls one by one. As Paige gazed back at her, the kitten blinked and Paige was suddenly reminded of the kitten in Lavinia Charm's portrait. The one she thought had blinked at her on her first day at the school. The damp kitten did look awfully like the one in the portrait, Paige thought. Could it be more than a coincidence, or was she just being silly?

As Paige watched Velvet thoughtfully, the kitten started purring contentedly and curled up on the quilt in a little furry ball. A few seconds later, she was fast asleep.

Chapter Five

"Come on, Paige," Shannon whispered. "Let's go. Is Velvet OK?"

Paige peered into the bag she was holding. Velvet was curled up comfortably on the cushion she'd put inside, and she gave a pleased little chirrup when she saw Paige looking in.

"She's fine," she whispered to Shannon.

They hurried down the first flight of stairs, Paige carrying the bag carefully. It was early the following day. The girls had managed to smuggle some tuna and a bit of cream out of the dining hall to feed Velvet the evening before, and she had slept on

Paige's bed all through the night. She'd been no trouble at all. But now they were going to release the kitten into the school grounds.

"My heart's thumping like crazy," Paige murmured to Shannon as they went down to the second floor. "We'll be in big trouble if we get caught!"

"Don't even go there," Shannon replied, trying to smile, but her face was pale with tension. Then she gave a little gasp and grabbed Paige's arm. "Someone's coming!"

Paige and Shannon whisked out of sight behind a stone pillar. Holding the bag protectively against her, Paige tried to breathe normally, but her knees were trembling like jelly.

"They've gone," Shannon whispered as the footsteps died away. "Come on, let's get out of here!"

The girls had decided to smuggle the kitten out of school while everyone else was safely in the dining hall at breakfast. Summer had gone on ahead of Paige and Shannon to check that the coast was clear. Now Paige could see Summer at the bottom of the last flight of stairs, beckoning to them.

"We haven't got much time or we'll be late for breakfast, and someone is bound to notice," she said urgently as Paige and Shannon drew level. "But it should be safe now, most people are already in the canteen."

The three girls hurried over to the huge oak door, and Paige let out an enormous sigh of relief as Shannon reached for the big iron handle. They'd made it!

"Where are you going?" demanded a sharp voice from behind them, making all three girls jump. "It's time for breakfast – didn't you hear the bell?"

"Abigail, must you always be so nosy?" sighed Shannon, spinning round to face the other girl.

"Well, where are you going?" Abigail demanded suspiciously, coming down the stairs towards them. "You'll be late for breakfast. You must be up to something."

"No, we're not." Paige glared at her, hoping Velvet wouldn't make a noise.

"Yes, you are!" Abigail retorted. She stared at them hard, eyes narrowed. Paige stood up straight and stared back at her, praying that Abigail would give up and leave them alone.

Abigail glanced down. "What's in the bag?" she asked curiously, looking even more suspicious.

"Nothing!" snapped Summer.

Abigail raised her eyebrows in a very superior manner. "Oh, *p-lease!*" she scoffed. "You should be at breakfast, but instead you're sneaking outside with a bag with *nothing* in it? Do you think I'm an idiot?"

"Well, now you come to mention it—" Shannon began.

Abigail flushed bright red with rage. "Let me see inside that bag!" she demanded.

Paige swallowed hard, trying not to look panicked, but inside her tummy was churning. Abigail would so *love* to get them into trouble, and this would be trouble with a capital T.

Shannon sighed loudly. "OK, Abigail, you win," she said, as Paige and Summer stared at her in dismay. "There's a mouse in the bag!"

Oh, great idea, Shannon! Paige thought with a rush of relief.

But Abigail wasn't looking at all convinced.

"I don't believe you!" she snapped. Suddenly she reached out and snatched the bag, taking Paige completely by surprise.

"Give that back!" Paige cried desperately. But Abigail was already peering eagerly inside.

"Look, there's no point in reporting us, Abigail," Summer said quickly. "We were just about to let her go, anyway . . ."

But Abigail was ignoring Summer and still staring into the bag. Suddenly she looked up with a dazed expression on her face. "It *is* a mouse!"

she remarked dreamily, thrusting the bag back at Paige. Then, as the girls watched in amazement, Abigail wandered off slowly in the direction of the canteen.

"Well!" Paige exclaimed, shaking her head in wonder. "What happened there? Abigail looks like she's been hypnotized or something!"

"Weird!" said Summer, looking confused. "I suppose Abigail must have spotted Velvet moving, and assumed she was a mouse."

"Unless Velvet hypnotized her," Shannon joked. "Come on, let's get out of here before whatever it is wears off!"

Paige and Summer both nodded enthusiastically as Shannon opened the door.

"That was far too close for comfort," Paige murmured. "I really thought we were done for when Abigail turned up!"

The girls hurried across the lawn and behind one of the old oak trees, where the broad trunk hid them from view. Then Paige opened the bag and lifted Velvet out.

"I wish we could keep her," she sighed.

"We *can't*," Shannon said, trying to sound firm

although she looked rather sad too. "We don't know where Velvet's from. She may have an owner who's really worried."

"You're right, Shannon," Paige agreed. "But we'll still miss her. Goodbye, Velvet," she said, planting a kiss on the kitten's head. "Go straight home now."

Summer and Shannon gathered round to stroke the kitten. Then Paige put her down on the grass and backed slowly away. She swallowed hard. Summer already had tears in her eyes and Shannon was looking a little too determinedly cheerful.

"Off you go then, Velvet," Paige said to the kitten, who sat looking up at her with quizzical golden eyes. "Take care."

The three girls turned and hurried away. But Paige couldn't resist one last look back over her shoulder.

"She's following us!" she exclaimed.

Summer and Shannon turned to see Velvet trotting after them, waving her tail from side to side.

Shannon immediately picked her up and put her back behind the oak tree. "Stay!" she said.

"She's not a dog, Shannon," Summer pointed out.

The girls started to walk off again, but exactly

the same thing happened. Velvet immediately set off after them, picking her way carefully across the grass.

"I know," said Shannon. "Let's distract her and then hide behind the tree. She'll soon go home if she can't see us."

Paige found a smooth white pebble and rolled it across the grass. Velvet bounded after it, and while the kitten wasn't looking, the girls rushed behind the oak tree. They flattened themselves against the trunk and waited.

Shannon peered round the tree. "She's gone," she said, sounding a little disappointed.

Miaow!

All three girls jumped and looked down. Velvet had come round behind the tree and was now sitting at Paige's feet.

Paige began to laugh. "It doesn't look like Velvet's going anywhere!" she pointed out. "What are we going to do?"

Summer knelt down on the grass in front of Velvet. "Look, Velvet," she said gently. "We'd love you to stay with us, but you simply *can't*. You have to go back to your owner, whoever that is."

"I don't think she can understand what you're saying, Summer," Shannon said.

Velvet put her tiny furry head on one side and placed one paw on Summer's knee.

"Oh, I don't know," said Paige. "Velvet *looks* like she's listening."

At that moment a white butterfly fluttered by. Velvet caught sight of it and raced away from the girls, following the butterfly across the lawns and into the woodland.

"Goodbye, Velvet!" Paige called, trying to blink away the tears in her eyes.

"That's it," Shannon said flatly, as Velvet disappeared into the trees. "She's gone."

"We'd better go to breakfast," Summer said quietly.

The girls trailed back into school in silence. They didn't say much over breakfast, and they didn't eat much either. Paige didn't feel hungry at all. They'd only had Velvet for a short time, but Paige was already missing her. She just hoped the kitten found her way safely back to her owner.

"We *had* to let Velvet go," Shannon said as they made their way back upstairs to the dorm after breakfast "We couldn't have kept her, could we?"

"No," Paige agreed, and Summer shook her head.

"I'm sure her owner will be really pleased to see her," Shannon went on, biting her lip.

"Yes," Summer said sadly. "Velvet's a gorgeous kitten."

Shannon opened the dorm door. "So we've done the right thing then," she sighed.

"Oh, yes," Paige replied. "It's just that now we'll probably never see Velvet again . . ."

The girls went into the dorm and then all three stopped short, because there, on Paige's bed, sat Velvet! She was grooming herself with her rough little pink tongue and, as the girls walked in, she looked up and gave a little trill of welcome, then went right back to washing her face with her paw.

"Velvet!" Paige gasped. She, Shannon and Summer dashed across the room. Paige scooped the kitten up and gave her a big cuddle. Velvet purred contentedly and curled up in Paige's arms, as Shannon and Summer stroked her.

"How *did* she get back in here?" Summer cried. "Look, the windows are closed!"

"One of them *must* have been open for Velvet to

get back in," said Shannon. "The wind probably blew it shut."

Paige frowned. She couldn't remember any of the windows being open before they'd gone down to breakfast. They'd kept them closed the night before because it had been quite a breezy evening after the storm. *Something very odd is going on*, Paige thought. *I'm sure there's more to Velvet than meets the eye* . . .

"We *can't* get rid of her now," Summer was saying. "She doesn't seem to have a home or an owner."

"Well, I suppose we'll just have to keep her until she's ready to leave for herself!" Shannon replied with a huge grin.

"Funny, that's just what I was thinking!" Paige laughed, looking thrilled. "Wow, our very own secret pet! That's even better than a midnight feast!"

Summer was also smiling from ear to ear.

"It's a big secret to keep," she pointed out, "but we can do it!"

"And Velvet's worth it!" added Paige.

"Our dorm isn't very close to any of the others, so nobody will hear her," Shannon said thoughtfully. "And *we'll* be able to hear if anyone comes up those creaky old stairs, so we'll have plenty of time to hide Velvet if necessary."

"We can smuggle food out of the dining hall for her," Summer put in eagerly. "And we can buy catfood when we go to the village shop."

"And we can ask our parents to put tins of tuna in our food parcels as a special treat for her," added Paige, placing Velvet gently on the bed.

Shannon laughed. "Our mums and dads are going to wonder what's going on," she said. "Usually we ask for cakes, biscuits and sweets!"

"We'd better find Velvet some toys too," Summer added.

Velvet seemed to be listening very attentively to their conversation, because she was watching them with her ears pricked. Blinking her huge golden eyes, she nuzzled Paige's hand with her soft pink nose, and bounded over to Shannon for a kiss. Then she patted Summer's knee with her paw.

Shannon laughed. "Velvet, you're officially our new roommate!" she announced.

Chapter Six

"Look!" Paige put down her knife and fork and pointed out of the dining hall window. "I don't believe it – there's Velvet *again!*"

Summer and Shannon swung round to look. The little black kitten was padding across the lawn in the evening sun. As the girls watched, Velvet bounced over to a stray leaf and began batting it playfully back and forth.

"Isn't she amazing?" Shannon laughed as Velvet chased the leaf out of sight behind a large rhododendron bush. "You never know where she's going to turn up next. She pops up all over the place!"

Paige nodded. "I know we leave the window open for her, but we *still* have no idea how she manages to get up and down from the roof," she pointed out. "I saw her outside the science lab the other day."

"And she was near the tennis courts yesterday," added Summer. "She was playing with an old tennis ball!"

"Velvet comes and goes as she pleases," Shannon said, shaking her head in admiration. "She's the boss!"

It was a week since the girls had tried to release Velvet in the school grounds. During that time the kitten had settled in very happily at Charm Hall, and now the girls couldn't imagine life without her. She roamed around outside for most of the day, and at night she slept on one or other of the girls' beds. At the bottom of the school drive there was a little village shop which the Charm Hall students were allowed to visit after lessons were over. Shannon, Summer and Paige had stocked up on catfood, but they also liked to bring Velvet little treats from the dining hall, although it wasn't always easy to sneak food out with dinner ladies and teachers around.

"I wonder if there's any fish left," Shannon said thoughtfully, as she finished off her meal. She glanced around the dining hall which was almost empty. "Dinner's nearly over. Maybe I can try and get some leftovers for Velvet. Come with me, Paige. If there's two of us asking, we might get a bit more!"

"Good luck!" grinned Summer, who was still finishing her pudding.

Paige followed Shannon across the dining hall to the serving hatch. Most of the dinner ladies were stacking the dishwashers and clearing up at the back of the kitchen. But one of them was still at the hatch, serving the last few puddings.

"Hello," Shannon said brightly. "I just wanted to say that the fish we had today was the best I've ever tasted!"

The dinner lady looked rather surprised, and Paige had to bite her lip to stop herself from laughing – the fish hadn't been *that* good.

"Really?" The dinner lady, whose name badge said *Joan*, asked doubtfully. She had curly grey hair, blue eyes and a round face.

"Yes, really!" Shannon said enthusiastically.

"My friend and I were wondering if there was any left over."

Joan frowned. "You mean you want seconds?" she asked, raising her eyebrows. "Most of the girls come back for extra chips or pudding – not *fish!*"

"Oh, I love fish," Shannon said eagerly. "It's my favourite food, and it's so healthy!"

Joan folded her arms and stared sternly at Shannon. Paige began to feel rather nervous.

"Now, aren't you the very same girl who came up to the hatch for your dinner about half an hour ago and said 'Oh, no, not fish again!'?" she asked coolly. "I was serving the potatoes, and I heard you with my own ears!"

Shannon looked flustered. "Well . . . er . . ." she stuttered. "That was *before* I tasted it!"

Paige bit her lip. She didn't think Joan was going to be convinced, but to her relief Joan's face suddenly broke into a big smile.

"Come on, girls," she chuckled, "I wasn't born yesterday! Why don't you tell me what's *really* going on?"

Paige and Shannon exchanged a look and Paige came to a decision. She would tell Joan the truth – just not the whole truth!

"The fish is for a little black kitten, who we call Velvet," Paige confessed, as Shannon stared at her in shock. "She's around the school grounds quite a lot and we wanted to feed her."

"Oh, yes." Joan nodded, her grey curls bouncing. "I've seen her a few times. She's lovely, isn't she? So friendly!" She winked at the girls. "Wait here."

"Phew!" Shannon said as Joan went off into the kitchens. "That was close. I thought Joan was going to come after us with her fish slice at one point!"

"I know," Paige laughed. "You did go a bit over the top with all that 'Oh, I love fish' and 'it's so healthy' stuff!"

Shannon laughed. "Well, it was worth a try!"

Joan hurried back to the hatch, a plastic sandwich bag in her hand. She passed it over to Shannon. "There you are," she said with a smile. "Just ask me if you want any leftovers in future."

"Thanks," Shannon said gratefully.

As Paige and Shannon turned away from the hatch, they saw that Abigail Carter was standing behind them, scraping the leftovers off her plate into one of the bins.

"What's that for?" she asked curiously, nodding at the sandwich bag. "It looks like fish."

"You win first prize, Abigail," said Shannon airily as they walked past her. "Go to the top of the class!"

Summer had just finished her pudding. She looked at the plastic bag in Shannon's hand in surprise.

"Velvet's going to have a feast tonight!" Paige laughed.

Summer smiled. "Can we stop off at the JCR before we go back to the dorm?" she asked as they left the dining hall. "The other day I noticed that one of the ping-pong balls has a big dent in the side. It's no good for table-tennis, but it'll be perfect for Velvet to play with."

"Good idea," Paige and Shannon agreed.

The JCR was very busy. All of the table-tennis tables were in use, and Abigail was on one of them, playing against her roommate, Mia, but no one was using the dented ball. Summer slipped it into her pocket.

When the girls got back to the dorm, they found Velvet lying on Summer's bed. She was stretched out on her back, paws in the air, fast asleep.

"She must have had a hard day chasing mice!" Shannon laughed.

Velvet opened her eyes slowly, yawned and rolled over. Then she climbed to her feet and jumped off the bed to bound over to them.

"I've got something for you, Velvet," said Summer, taking the ping-pong ball from her pocket and rolling it across the carpet.

Velvet raced after it and nudged it with her tiny nose. The ball was so light she could move it easily and with a mew of delight, she dashed after it again. The ball clattered and bounced off the beds and desks as Velvet chased it around the room.

"Shall we give her the fish now?" Shannon asked, untying the plastic bag.

But just then, without any warning, the door burst open. Paige, Shannon and Summer froze, and Velvet, who was still chasing the ping-pong ball across the carpet, stopped and looked up, her golden eyes alert.

"A kitten!" Abigail Carter gasped, her face alight with triumph as she stood in the doorway. "I *knew* you were up to something. I just knew it!"

Chapter Seven

Paige was so shocked, she could hardly speak. She realized that the noise of the ping-pong ball bouncing around meant they hadn't heard Abigail's approach, and of all the girls in the school to find out about Velvet, Abigail was certainly the worst! Paige knew that this meant only one thing: they wouldn't be allowed to keep Velvet, and the kitten would have to go.

Summer was also lost for words, but Shannon stepped forward confidently.

"OK, Abigail," she said, holding up her hands. "You caught us fair and square. Although you *do* seem to have forgotten that there's a school rule about knocking before you enter someone else's dorm."

Abigail raised her eyebrows. "I came to get some school property back," she said. "I'm one of the JCR monitors and you're not supposed to take any of the equipment away without permission!"

"You mean the dented ping-pong ball?" Paige asked in amazement. That was *so* obviously just an excuse!

"Yes, I saw you take it!" Abigail said haughtily. "And anyway, I don't think anyone's really going to care about me not knocking on your door. Not when *you're* breaking the school rules by keeping a pet in your room!"

"Oh, come on, Abigail!" said Shannon, and Paige could see that her friend was trying to keep her cool. "We're not keeping Velvet here. She just visits us every so often, that's all. Just walk away and forget you ever saw her."

"Oh I couldn't possibly do *that!*" Abigail said smugly. She folded her arms and stared triumphantly at the girls. "I simply *have* to report this. Now let me see, it's Mrs Bloomfield's evening off, isn't it? So who's on duty tonight?" She stroked her chin, pretending to think. "Oh, yes!" Her eyes gleamed wickedly. "It's Mrs Stark."

Paige, Summer and Shannon glanced at each other in dismay. They were in deep, deep trouble.

"Look, Abigail," Paige said, picking Velvet up and holding her out to the other girl. "Isn't she cute?"

"And she's ever so quiet," Summer chimed in. "Nobody will know she's here if you don't tell."

Velvet stretched out one of her soft paws towards Abigail. Abigail hesitated, and the smug look on her face disappeared for a second, but then she pulled abruptly away from the kitten.

"Keep it away from me," she snapped. "I don't like cats." She spun round and went over to the door. "And now, if you've finished begging, I'm going to find Mrs Stark and tell here exactly what's going on here!" And throwing one last infuriating smile over her shoulder at Paige, Shannon and Summer, she clattered off down the creaky stairs.

"That's it then," Summer said in a shaky voice. "We won't be able to keep Velvet."

"Maybe if we speak to Miss Linnet—" Paige began, stroking Velvet.

But Shannon was shaking her head. "Miss Linnet won't make an exception for us," she said sadly. "If she did, all the girls would want pets!"

"We've got to do something!" Paige said desperately. "We can't just let Mrs Stark take Velvet away."

"Maybe we could hide Velvet and try to convince Mrs Stark that Abigail got her facts wrong," Summer suggested.

"That's our only hope," Shannon agreed, pushing the bag of fish into her pocket out of sight. "Quick, Summer, open your wardrobe!"

Summer pulled open the wardrobe doors as they heard footsteps coming up the stairs. Carefully she used a pile of sweaters to make a cosy nest for the kitten, then Paige kissed the top of Velvet's head and placed her in the wardrobe.

"*Please* be quiet, Velvet!" she begged.

Miaow, Velvet responded as Summer closed the wardrobe doors.

A moment later the dorm door opened and Mrs Stark strode into the room, followed by a grinning

Abigail. Mrs Stark was a tall woman with grey hair and silver-rimmed glasses. She hardly ever seemed to smile, but Paige's heart sank as she saw the grim look on the teacher's face; she looked even more forbidding than usual.

Mrs Stark came to a stop in the middle of the room and raised her eyebrows. "Abigail Carter tells me that you have secretly been keeping a *kitten* in your room!" She glared at them. "You know the school rules! Where *is* this kitten, and what do you three have to say for yourselves?"

Shannon, Summer and Paige stood silently, heads bent. Paige's tongue felt heavy in her mouth. She couldn't say a thing.

"*Atishoo!*" Mrs Stark sneezed suddenly, breaking the silence. She pulled a handkerchief out of her pocket. "*Atishoo!*"

"Bless you, Mrs Stark," Shannon said politely, "but can you *see* a kitten here?"

Paige bit her lip. Of course Mrs Stark couldn't *see* a kitten at the moment because Velvet was in the wardrobe. But would the teacher accept that she'd made a mistake and go away?

"No!" Mrs Stark snapped. "But I'm allergic to

cats – *atishoo* – and ever since I walked in here I've been sneezing!"

Paige's heart sank right down into her shoes as Abigail's grin got wider.

"They must have hidden the kitten when I came to fetch you, Mrs Stark," Abigail suggested eagerly. "Shall I help you look for it?"

"I'm quite capable of finding a kitten by myself, thank you, Abigail," Mrs Stark said coolly. She went over to the girls' beds and knelt to look underneath. When the teacher's back was turned, Shannon pulled a face at Abigail who simply smirked back at her.

Paige, Summer and Shannon watched as Mrs Stark searched the room from top to bottom. She left the wardrobes till last. Paige had a lump in her throat when, finally, Mrs Stark opened the doors of Summer's wardrobe.

Sneezing again, Mrs Stark began to poke around at the bottom of the wardrobe. Paige held her breath. Any minute she expected to see Velvet's head pop out of the sweaters. Her heart thumped against her ribs.

Mrs Stark took one last long look around the

wardrobe. "Well, there doesn't appear to be anything here," she said at last.

Paige was stunned. In fact, she was so shocked, she had to stop herself from saying *But there must be!* She glanced at Shannon and Summer and saw that they both looked as surprised as she felt. Where was Velvet?

"But the kitten must be here somewhere," Abigail said with a frown. She wasn't looking half so pleased with herself now, Paige noted. "I *saw* it!"

Mrs Stark still looked very suspicious as she closed the wardrobe doors. "I'm not happy about this," she said furiously, staring hard at Paige, Summer and Shannon. "I'm not happy about this at all. I am *convinced* that there has been a kitten in this room!"

Paige tried to look innocent as Mrs Stark's eyes bored into hers.

"This is a warning," Mrs Stark snapped, "so make sure you listen very carefully to what I say. If I discover that a cat has *ever* set foot in this dorm, you will all be in very, very serious trouble."

She turned and swept over to the door, stopping to glare at Abigail. "Please be sure of your facts before you come to me with a story like this in future, Abigail," she said frostily.

"But there *was* a kitten, Mrs Stark!" Abigail muttered, pouting sulkily as she followed the teacher out into the corridor. "It must be in their dorm *somewhere.*"

"Abigail, the kitten's certainly not here now!" Mrs Stark retorted. "And I don't have any more time for this nonsense. But since you obviously have too much time on your hands, you can come and tidy the maths cupboard for me."

Their voices died away as they made their way down the stairs.

"Velvet is safe and Abigail's getting it in the neck," Shannon observed with a grin. "I don't think my day could get any better!"

"It serves Abigail right," Summer said indignantly, "for trying to get Velvet kicked out. Don't you think so, Paige?"

"Yes," Paige agreed distractedly, staring at the wardrobe in confusion. "But where *is* Velvet?"

Chapter Eight

"Good question!" Shannon said, looking anxious.

Summer ran over to her wardrobe and pulled the doors open. As Paige looked inside, she thought she glimpsed a strange golden shimmer, but she forgot all about that when she saw that, sitting exactly where they had left her, among the sweaters, was Velvet herself.

Paige, Summer and Shannon stared at the kitten in stunned disbelief, as Velvet mewed a greeting. Then, looking completely calm, she stuck one paw behind her ear and gave herself a good scratch.

"This is weird!" Summer gasped. "Mrs Stark

searched the wardrobe. We saw her!"

"Maybe there's a hole in the back and Velvet climbed through it," Shannon suggested.

Velvet stopped scratching, leaped lightly off the pile of sweaters and padded over to Paige's bed. Meanwhile Shannon got down on her hands and knees and felt around at the back of the wardrobe. "No hole!" she announced, looking puzzled.

Velvet was now lying on her back on Paige's patchwork quilt, enjoying a good stretch and a wriggle.

"Look!" Summer pointed at one of Velvet's front paws. "She's got a tiny patch of white there, just above her pad. I've never noticed it before, have you?"

Paige and Shannon shook their heads.

Summer studied the white patch more closely.

"It's shaped like a witch's hat," she announced.

Paige laughed. "Maybe Velvet's a witch cat!" she declared, only half joking as she remembered the faint golden shimmer she'd noticed in the wardrobe. "Maybe that's how she managed to fool Mrs Stark and disappear!"

Summer smiled, but Shannon stared

thoughtfully at Paige. "You know," she said, "there was a rumour about the women of the Charm family. People used to say they were witches!"

"You mean Lavinia Charm who founded the school might have been a *witch*?" asked Summer, raising her eyebrows in disbelief.

"Ooh, you know, there *is* a black kitten in her portrait," Paige mentioned.

Shannon shook her head. "No, not Lavinia," she said. "At least, I don't think so. This was hundreds of years ago." She touched Velvet's paw gently. "But maybe Velvet *is* a witch cat – or maybe she's descended from one!"

Paige frowned. "Do you think so, Shannon?" she asked.

"Maybe . . ." Shannon's voice trailed away uncertainly, and for a moment she didn't look her usual confident self. "I don't know. But I do think there's more to Velvet than meets the eye!"

Paige nodded. "Remember when Velvet turned up in our dorm after we tried to let her go in the grounds?" she said. "Well, I don't know how she got back in because I'm *sure* we didn't leave any of the windows open!"

Shannon's eyes began to sparkle with excitement. "See?" she said. "Magic! And don't forget when Abigail looked in our bag and thought she saw a mouse? Well, maybe Velvet's magic *had* hypnotized her!"

All three girls stared at Velvet, who was stretched out lazily on the bed.

"It's nearly time for lights out," Summer said, glancing at the clock. "We'd better get ready for bed or we'll definitely need magic to save us from Mrs Stark!"

"I'm too excited to sleep," Shannon laughed, grabbing her pink pyjamas. "Just think, we could have our very own witch cat!"

No talking was allowed after lights out, so the girls reluctantly said goodnight to each other and the dorm fell silent. As Paige slid under her duvet, she couldn't help thinking about Velvet. Could their little kitten *really* be a witch cat?

Paige glanced down at the end of her bed. In the moonlight she could see Velvet curled up on the duvet, gazing steadily back at her.

"*Are* you a witch cat, Velvet?" Paige whispered.

Velvet purred and blinked her golden eyes.

"Maybe, just *maybe*, you are," Paige murmured to the kitten. She felt her heart begin to beat faster with excitement, because if Velvet was, then there could be some magical times ahead for them all.

"You know what?" Shannon said, nudging Paige as they opened their French textbooks in the last lesson before lunch the following morning. "If looks could kill, you, me and Summer would be stretched out on the classroom floor!"

Paige glanced up. Abigail Carter was sitting at the next table, and she was glaring at them angrily.

"She's been doing it all morning," Paige whispered. "She's really got it in for us now!"

"We'll have to be careful then," Shannon went on, picking up her pen. "I bet Abigail's already planning her next raid on our dorm."

"I know we're not allowed to lock the door," Paige said thoughtfully, "but maybe we could rig up some sort of warning device?"

"Good idea!" said Summer eagerly. "Or we could try and wedge a book under the door or something to hold it closed. Then nobody would be able to burst in as quickly as Abigail did."

Shannon nodded and leaned forwards. "Did you think any more about what I said yesterday?" she asked in a low voice. "About Velvet being a witch cat?"

Before any of them could reply, Miss Olivier, the French teacher, looked round the room. *"Silence, s'il vous plait.* Get on with your translations," she said sharply.

Paige bent her head over her work. She'd thought about hardly anything else since their conversation the night before. She was sure that there was something extremely out of the ordinary about Velvet.

About ten minutes before the end of the lesson, one of the older girls brought a note to Miss Olivier.

The teacher read it. "Girls, we have to go to the assembly hall right away," she said, standing up. "Miss Linnet has an important announcement to make to us."

Everyone looked surprised.

"I wonder what this is all about," Shannon said thoughtfully as they put their books away and filed out of the classroom.

"Miss Olivier looked a bit serious, didn't she?" said Paige.

As the girls made their way into the assembly hall, Paige saw that the whole school was gathered there ready for Miss Linnet's announcement. Paige sat between Summer and Shannon, looking at the stage at the end of the room where Miss Linnet and the senior teachers usually sat.

In the middle of the stage today was an easel which held a large painting in a heavy golden frame. Paige was surprised to see that it was the portrait of Lavinia Charm from Miss Linnet's office. Paige thought that Lavinia looked proud and regal, although her blue eyes were kind, but what interested Paige far more was the jet-black kitten curled up on Lavinia's lap. Just as she had remembered, the kitten had golden eyes, but now Paige saw that she also had a plum-coloured collar.

Paige stifled a gasp of amazement. She hadn't really had much chance to study the portrait when she'd been in Miss Linnet's office that first day, but now she realized that the cat in the portrait looked *exactly* like Velvet!

Quickly she nudged Shannon and Summer.

"Look at the cat in the picture with Lavinia Charm," Paige whispered urgently. "Doesn't it look just like Velvet?"

Shannon and Summer stared at the portrait.

"It's *identical!*" Shannon said in a low voice. "It *is* Velvet!"

"How can it be?" Summer pointed out. "That portrait was painted when the school was founded, nearly a hundred years ago!"

"It *could* be Velvet," Paige murmured as Miss Linnet hurried into the hall. "*If* she's a witch cat. You see, I saw that portrait on my first day here. And the kitten in the picture actually blinked at me!"

"Are you sure?" Shannon asked eagerly. "Why didn't you say anything before?"

"I thought I must have imagined it," Paige replied. "But now I'm beginning to think that it was all to do with Velvet's magic."

"I'm still not sure that Velvet *can* be magical," Summer whispered. "But she does look just like the kitten in the picture. What do you think the portrait's doing here, anyway?"

There was no time for Paige or Shannon to answer because Miss Linnet had now walked on

70

to the stage. Silence fell around the room immediately.

"Girls," Miss Linnet began in a sombre tone. "This is a very sad day for us all. I never dreamed that the time would come when I would have to stand here and give you such dreadful news."

Paige glanced at Shannon and Summer, her eyes wide with surprise. Both of her friends looked equally confused. Miss Linnet sounded very serious.

"I think that Lavinia Charm would be very distressed, too, if she were here today," Miss Linnet went on, indicating the portrait. "She loved this school as much as we all do."

She stopped and Paige was horrified to see that there were tears in the headmistress's eyes.

"Girls," Miss Linnet said, her voice trembling, "I'm sorry to say that, in a few weeks' time, Charm Hall School must close for good!"

Chapter Nine

Paige was so shocked that for a moment she wondered if she was hearing things. Charm Hall School *closing*? But why? How? Shannon and Summer looked just as stunned as Paige and so did every single girl in the assembly hall.

"I don't believe it!" Shannon gasped as, after a moment's silence, everyone burst out talking at once.

"No, it's not possible!" Summer said, her face pale.

Paige didn't know what to say. She hadn't really wanted to come to Charm Hall at first, but now that she was here, she loved it. And what would happen to Velvet? It was the kitten's home too.

Miss Linnet held up a hand for silence. She swallowed hard and blinked away her tears. "I was just as shocked as you when I heard about this," she began. "We have already started contacting your parents to tell them what is happening, but perhaps it's best if I explain to you the exact circumstances which have led to this."

She took a deep breath. "Our founder, Lavinia Charm, originally set the school up with a one-hundred-year lease, so that at the end of the lease the property would once again revert back to the Charm family. However, over the years Lavinia became very attached to the school and decided that she wanted it to continue. So she made an addition to her will – what we call an addendum. The addendum left the house and the grounds to the school for ever. At least," Miss Linnet sighed deeply, "that was what everyone believed."

Paige listened, fascinated. *If Lavinia Charm had wanted the school to continue as it was, for ever, why did it have to close?* she wondered.

"The problem is that nobody can find the

addendum to Lavinia's will," Miss Linnet went on. "Lavinia insisted on keeping it rather than handing it over to her solicitors, and it hasn't been seen for years. It may have been accidentally destroyed or lost, or Lavinia may have just changed her mind, although . . ." Miss Linnet shook her head, ". . . I really do not believe that she would have done that."

Paige frowned. *What will happen to the school if we all have to leave?* she asked herself.

"This means that when the hundred years is up in just a few weeks' time, the house will no longer belong to the school, but will revert to Mr Oliver Charm, Lavinia's great-grandson," Miss Linnet went on. "A property developer has recently offered Mr Charm a large sum of money for the house and the grounds . . ."

"And Mr Charm wants to sell!" Shannon whispered furiously to Paige and Summer, unable to keep quiet any longer.

"The developer wants to turn the school into a five-star hotel and Mr Charm is keen to sell," Miss Linnet explained. "This is a very valuable site and the developers are eager to get their hands on it."

She gazed round the hall at everyone, lifting her chin proudly. "I know this is a huge shock to you all, as it was to me. But we mustn't forget that we always, *always* try to do our best at Charm Hall, whatever the circumstances. So let's make our last few weeks here a time to remember!"

Paige nodded along with everyone else, even though she still felt completely dazed.

"Now it's time for lunch, so off you all go," Miss Linnet said kindly. "And I'll give you more information about the closure of the school as soon as I have any."

Everyone began filing out of the hall in miserable silence. Some of the girls were crying.

"Oh, I don't believe it!" Paige burst out. "This is awful! We can't even stay till the end of this term."

"I'm sure Lavinia Charm wouldn't want the school to close," said Shannon sadly. "If only someone could find that add . . . whatever you call it."

"Addendum," Summer finished for her.

Most of the school had left the hall now, but Shannon wandered over to the stage to take a closer look at the portrait. Paige and Summer followed her.

"Look at that," Shannon whispered, pointing at the painted black kitten. "It *is* Velvet! I'm sure it is."

"The eyes are exactly the same colour," Paige agreed.

"And so is the collar," added Summer.

"What's going to happen to Velvet if the school closes?" Paige asked miserably. "She *belongs* here."

"Hurry up, girls," Miss Olivier said, coming over to them. "You should be on your way to the dining hall."

"I don't think I could eat a thing," Paige sighed, as they trailed out of the hall and along the corridor. She couldn't believe that just as she'd grown to love Charm Hall she would have to leave. What if she, Shannon and Summer ended up at different schools? They might never see each other, or Velvet, ever again!

"I'm not hungry either," Summer sighed.

"Nor me," Shannon added.

Even though it was a warm sunny day, nothing could lift the girls' mood. Even seeing her favourite dish, chicken pie and chips, on the lunch menu couldn't cheer Paige up.

"Hello, girls," Joan the dinner lady said, looking downcast. "Isn't it sad that the school's closing?"

"Yes, it is," sighed Paige. "I'll have chicken pie with my chips, please."

"I'm afraid the food isn't quite up to its usual standard today," Joan went on. "Everyone in the kitchen is so upset, we've been at sixes and sevens all morning." She inspected the pies closely and then popped one on to Paige's plate. "That one doesn't look too bad."

The girls took their trays to the picnic tables on the terrace outside the dining hall. A lot of the other girls were eating outside too, but there was none of the usual lunchtime chatter and laughter.

"Oh, this is horrible!" Shannon said, putting her tray down on an empty table. "I just wish there was something we could do."

"Like what?" Paige asked. She sat down, glad that they were right at the end of the terrace and that there was nobody else around. It was terrible to see everyone's sad faces.

"I don't know," Shannon muttered, "but we can't just let Charm Hall close, can we?"

Paige and Summer looked at each other in silence, and Shannon bit her lip.

"I know, I know," she said miserably, slumping down on to the bench. "There's nothing we can do about it, is there?" She picked up her knife and fork and popped a piece of cheese and ham pizza into her mouth.

Almost immediately, she pulled a face. "Yuk! The pizza's all soggy!"

Cautiously Paige took a bite of chicken pie. It was usually delicious, but not today. The pastry was burned around the edges, and instead of being soft and flaky it was rock hard.

"The mash on top of my shepherd's pie is all lumpy," Summer remarked, poking it with her fork. "The dinner ladies must have been really upset!"

Miaow!

Paige, Shannon and Summer jumped at the familiar sound. Velvet was padding her way towards them, tail curling high over her back in greeting.

"Hello, Velvet," Paige said, trying to smile. Normally, she'd have been delighted to see the kitten, but today all she could do was worry about what would happen to Velvet when the school closed.

"How *do* you get up and down from the school roof, Velvet?" Summer was asking curiously.

The kitten trotted over, sprang lightly up on to the picnic table and stared at the girls with her warm golden gaze.

"You know we should probably try and eat something. We've got PE next," Shannon pointed out. "Maybe some of the pizza is OK."

"I'll scrape the mashed potato off mine and just eat the mince," said Summer.

Paige put down her knife and fork. She wasn't hungry at all. Velvet patted her arm with one paw and Paige turned slightly so that she could stroke the kitten. As she did so, she was amazed to see a faint golden shimmer appear around Velvet's nose. The golden gleam rippled out along the kitten's whiskers and Paige was reminded of the same golden glimmer she had noticed in the wardrobe the evening Velvet had hidden from Mrs Stark.

Paige blinked. Was she seeing things? Was it simply a trick of the light because the sun was so bright? Or could it really be *magic*? She glanced at Shannon and Summer, but they were both inspecting their food and didn't seem to have noticed anything.

"Velvet, what are you up to?" Paige whispered, putting out her hand to touch the kitten's whiskers lightly. But the shimmer of gold had vanished as quickly as it had appeared.

"I think she's knows we're miserable," said Shannon, "and she's come to cheer us up. Velvet, if you *are* a witch cat, can you please do something to help us? Maybe you could hypnotize Mr Charm or something . . ."

Shannon sighed and popped another piece of soggy pizza into her mouth. But as she chewed, a puzzled expression spread across her face. "This is weird!" she exclaimed. "My pizza suddenly tastes delicious!"

Chapter Ten

Paige and Summer stared at Shannon in disbelief.

"You just said it was all soggy!" Summer reminded her.

"It isn't now," Shannon said enthusiastically. "The base is crisp and the cheese is all hot and melting. Yum!"

Paige glanced down at her chicken pie. To her surprise, it looked completely different. The burned bits had vanished and the pastry looked softer and flakier. Paige took a bite. "Mine tastes different, too!" she announced. "It's lovely!"

"Try yours, Summer," Shannon said eagerly.

Summer ate a forkful of mash from the top of her shepherd's pie. "The lumps have all gone!" she gasped in disbelief.

Shannon stared at Velvet as the kitten jumped down from the picnic table and padded across Paige's lap towards her.

"Velvet, did *you* have anything to do with this?" asked Shannon suspiciously.

The kitten's eyes were half closed as she clambered on to Shannon's lap and sat down purring contentedly.

Paige hesitated. "I did see something rather strange," she said slowly. "Did either of you two notice?"

Shannon and Summer shook their heads.

"What did you see, Paige?" Summer asked curiously.

"Was it something to do with Velvet?" Shannon added.

Paige nodded. Quickly she described the magical golden shimmer she'd seen around Velvet's whiskers.

"Oh!" Shannon cried happily. "I knew it! Velvet *is* magic!"

"Do you really think so?" Summer asked doubtfully.

"Yes, I do," Shannon said, and Paige nodded in agreement. Meanwhile, Velvet jumped down and trotted off to investigate a nearby bush.

The girls tucked into their food happily now, marvelling at the fact that it was suddenly so tasty. But, a few minutes later, Penny hurried over to them.

"Paige, you've got to go to the school office," she said. "Your mum's on the phone."

"Oh!" Paige jumped to her feet. She guessed that her mum was phoning to talk about the closure of Charm Hall. It was very unusual for a pupil to get a telephone call via the school office. Usually calls came in on the payphones in the entrance hall.

Paige suddenly felt miserable again. For a few brief moments, the thought that Velvet really could be magic had made her forget about the fact that the school was closing, but the phone call brought it all flooding back.

"We'll meet you later," Shannon said quietly.

Paige nodded and ran off.

The school office was next to Miss Linnet's

study. Paige knocked and hurried inside.

Mrs Vernon, the school secretary, was typing at the computer. "Ah, Paige," she said briskly. "You can take your call on that phone over by the window."

Paige picked up the receiver. "Hello, Mum?"

"Hello, darling," her mum replied.

Paige smiled. Her mum sounded so clear, it was almost like she was in the next room, and it was always great to hear her voice.

"How are you?" her mum continued. "We had a call this morning to say that the school is closing quite soon."

"Yes," Paige said sadly. "And it's awful! I love it here."

"I'm so sorry, darling," her mum said sympathetically. "But the thing is, we've found a school here in Dubai which we think you'll like."

"Oh, really?" Paige said. She tried to sound enthusiastic, but it was difficult because the only school she wanted to go to was Charm Hall.

"Yes, so we were wondering if you wanted to come over right away," Mrs Hart went on. "There's half of the summer term left so you could start school here immediately and you won't have missed much. There doesn't seem to be much point in you staying at Charm Hall right to the end."

Paige was silent. Her mother's words made it all feel so real. Charm was closing. She would have to leave and, really, her mother was right, there wasn't much point in staying on at Charm Hall when she could be settling into a new school in Dubai.

But even as she had that thought, Paige realized that logic didn't matter. She wanted to see her mum and dad, but more than that, she wanted to stay with Summer and Shannon and Velvet. She wasn't about to leave Charm Hall and her new friends until she had to.

"Mum, would you mind very much if I stayed on until the school closes?" she asked. "I know it's not for long, but I've made some really good friends here."

"Of course you can stay," Mrs Hart replied quickly. "If that's what you want."

"Thanks, Mum," Paige said gratefully.

They chatted for a few more minutes and then Paige hung up. She hurried out of the school office to find Shannon and Summer waiting for her.

"What happened to Velvet?" Paige asked.

"She's gone off on her mysterious travels again," Summer said. "Has your mum heard about the school closing?"

Paige nodded. "She asked me to go to Dubai straight away," Paige told her friends. "They've found a school for me."

Shannon and Summer looked horrified.

"When are you going?" Summer asked sadly.

Paige shook her head. "You don't get rid of me that easily. I'm not going anywhere!" she said fiercely. "Not until the school closes, anyway. I asked my mum if I could stay and she agreed."

"Well," Summer said, shaking her head at Paige in mock anger, "thanks for giving us a big fright!"

"Sorry!" Paige grinned and glanced at Shannon, who gave her a faint smile in return. She looked very downcast, and Paige frowned. "You're very quiet, Shannon. Are you OK?"

Shannon shook her head. "Not really," she said in a shaky voice. "While you were in the office, I got a text from my mum and dad about the school closing." She held up her mobile phone. "Remember I told you they were working out in Angola?"

Paige nodded. Shannon had told her before about her parents, who were both doctors. She'd also explained that she couldn't visit them in Angola because parts of the African country were so dangerous. So her mum or her dad travelled back to England every school holiday to spend time with Shannon at the family home.

"So what did your mum and dad say?" asked Paige. "Is one of them coming back to take you home when the school closes?"

Shannon bit her lip. "That's just it," she said miserably. "They can't come back until the summer holidays." She looked so upset that Paige began to feel quite alarmed. "They said that when the school closes, I've got to go and stay with great-aunt Agnes!"

"Who?" Paige asked, puzzled.

"She's horrible!" Shannon burst out. "I stayed with her last February half-term when Mum and Dad couldn't get a flight home. She lives in this great big house out in the middle of nowhere, and it's *freezing*! She's so mean, she won't put the central heating on or let me use the phone or anything – she says it costs too much. I offered to pay for my phone calls but she still wouldn't let me call anyone and my mobile won't work there because there's no signal."

Paige was staring at her friend in disbelief. "She sounds awful!" she said sympathetically.

"Oh, she is!" Shannon groaned. "I told Summer all about her when I got back to school."

Summer nodded. "Shannon had to sleep in this tiny, cold attic at the top of the house, and great-aunt Agnes made her do loads of cleaning," Summer put in.

"She's so fussy, she drives me crazy!" Shannon said gloomily. "Oh, I can't *believe* this is happening!"

"I'll ask my parents if you can come and stay with us for a few days," suggested Summer.

Shannon smiled weakly. "Thanks," she said, "but great-aunt Agnes won't let me go out when I'm staying with her. She's too mean to drive me anywhere!"

Paige and Summer glanced at each other in silence. Paige didn't know *what* to say. She felt so sorry for Shannon, but the school was closing and there was nothing they could do about it.

* * *

"Don't the gardens look gorgeous?" Paige said to Summer and Shannon. Then she sighed. "I can't bear to think of the school being turned into a hotel!"

It was later that day, after study hour, and the girls had some free time before dinner. Because it had been such a warm day, they were enjoying a game of Frisbee in the cool evening air. The sun was setting slowly overhead, and the sky was streaked with pink and gold. Butterflies danced among the flower beds, while bees buzzed here and there.

"There's Miss Linnet," Shannon said, catching the Frisbee with a leap.

Paige turned and saw the headmistress walking through the gardens.

"Miss Linnet's looked so sad all day," Summer said quietly. "It must be awful for her."

Suddenly Shannon gave a gasp. "Look!" She pointed towards the woodland at the edge of the lawn. "It's Velvet."

Paige stared, unable to believe her eyes. They had left the little black kitten asleep upstairs on Summer's bed. But now Velvet was emerging from the trees and bounding across the lawn towards Miss Linnet.

"Quick! We've got to head her off before she

reaches Miss Linnet," Shannon said, taking off across the lawn.

Paige and Summer followed. Paige's heart was beating like a drum. She just hoped Miss Linnet didn't think Velvet was a stray and decide to take her to an animal shelter!

The girls were quick, but they were too far away from Miss Linnet to reach her before Velvet did. Paige saw Velvet gently wind herself around the headteacher's ankles.

Miss Linnet jumped and looked down. "Oh!" she gasped.

"Too late," Shannon groaned, coming to a halt so abruptly that Paige and Summer almost cannoned into her.

They were a couple of metres away from Miss Linnet now, and Paige watched as the headmistress bent to stroke the kitten. Velvet's tail had begun to twitch in a very strange way, flicking slowly and rhythmically from side to side like the pendulum of a clock.

"And where have you come from?" Miss Linnet said kindly, picking Velvet up and cuddling her against her shoulder. The kitten peeped mischievously over the headmistress's shoulder at the girls, blinking her large eyes.

Paige heard Summer gasp, and she knew why. The magical, golden glow she'd seen before was shimmering across Velvet's whiskers in waves, making them glitter and vibrate.

Her heart thudding with excitement, Paige glanced at her friends. Miss Linnet couldn't see what was happening because Velvet was facing them. But Shannon and Summer had definitely noticed this time. They stood transfixed, with looks of amazement on their faces.

After a moment or two the golden glimmer disappeared. Miss Linnet gave Velvet a final stroke and put her gently down on the grass. Velvet gave a little mew and then trotted off again, vanishing into the flower border near to where the headmistress was standing.

As Miss Linnet turned to watch her go, she noticed Paige, Summer and Shannon. "Did you see that beautiful kitten, girls?" she called. "I expect it came from the farm down the lane."

"Yes, Miss Linnet," Summer agreed, sounding very relieved.

"We'd better go inside," said Paige quickly. She was longing for a chance to discuss what had just happened with Summer and Shannon. "It's nearly dinner time."

"Are you coming to dinner, Miss Linnet?" asked Shannon politely.

The headteacher didn't answer. She was frowning hard and seemed lost in thought.

"Miss Linnet?" Shannon said. "Are you OK?"

Miss Linnet smiled suddenly. "I'm sorry, girls," she replied, "but I've been walking the grounds for the last hour, wondering how on earth I'm going to get the whole of Charm Hall cleared during the next few weeks, and I've just had a wonderful idea!"

"What's that?" Paige asked eagerly.

"Founder's Day is coming up, and we always celebrate it in style," Miss Linnet said firmly. "Well, since this will be our last one, I think we should make it the best Founder's Day ever," she went on. "So we'll empty Charm Hall from top to bottom, and have a big fête and a jumble sale!"

"That sounds like fun!" Summer cried, and Paige and Shannon nodded eagerly.

"And we'll give the money we make to charity,"

the headmistress said thoughtfully. "Then at least *someone* will benefit from this horrible situation. I'm going to start planning it right away!" And she hurried off towards the school.

Immediately Shannon spun round and grinned at Paige and Summer. "Paige, you were right about that magical shimmer!" she exclaimed. "Summer and I just saw it around Velvet's whiskers. It was just like you described."

Paige nodded. "And then Miss Linnet had her brilliant idea," she added. "I'm *sure* that was because of Velvet's magic."

Summer frowned. "I don't know," she said slowly. "That golden glow could just have been the sunlight reflecting off Velvet's whiskers. And Miss Linnet having her idea at the same time could just have been a coincidence."

"Oh, Summer!" Shannon groaned, smiling at her friend. "Well, you can believe what you like. *I* believe that Velvet is a witch cat!"

So do I! Paige thought. *And maybe we'll be able to convince Summer too. If we have enough time before the school closes . . .*

Chapter Eleven

"So how many white elephants do you think we'll find around Charm Hall?" Shannon joked with Paige and Summer as they hurried down the stairs towards the ground floor.

Paige was confused. "What are you talking about?" she asked. "There aren't any elephants at Charm Hall!"

Summer laughed. "Take no notice of Shannon," she told Paige. "A white elephant stall is another name for a junk stall, that's all."

Before Paige could reply, there was a loud sigh from behind them.

"Honestly, Paige Hart!" said a scornful voice. "Fancy not knowing what a white elephant stall is!"

The girls turned to see Abigail Carter standing there in the corridor with the usual snooty look on her face.

"Abigail, didn't your parents ever tell you that it's rude to eavesdrop on other people's conversations?" asked Shannon.

"Not to mention bursting into their dorms unannounced," Paige added.

Abigail scowled. "I don't know what you did with that kitten," she muttered, "but if Mrs Stark catches you, you'll be in big trouble." She stared inquisitively at the girls. "So you're running the white elephant stall, are you?"

Summer nodded. "We asked Miss Linnet if we could, and she said yes."

Miss Linnet had announced her idea in assembly and had asked each year in the school to take on certain tasks at the fête. Paige's year were in charge of supplying and running the stalls. Each house would be responsible for a different one. The girls in Hummingbird House were given the job of collecting bric-a-brac and interesting objects from around the school for the white elephant stall. Since Paige, Summer and Shannon had volunteered to actually run the stall on the day, they had got permission from Miss Linnet to search the school cellars.

Nightingale, Peacock and Swan houses were running the book, bake and craft stalls. There would also be other activities such as a tombola, a lucky dip and competitions such as "guess the number of jelly beans in the jar" as well as a bouncy castle, a raffle and a refreshments tent.

"Well, Peacock are doing the bake stall, and *I've* volunteered to help to make cakes *and* to run the stall," Abigail said, raising her eyebrows in a superior manner. "We'll definitely make loads more money than you and your silly white elephants!"

"Oh, you think so?" Shannon replied. "Well, you know what this means, don't you?"

Abigail looked puzzled. "What?"

"War!" Shannon said bluntly. "We'll see who makes more money, you or us."

"Oh, great," Abigail replied, grinning in a very irritating way. "My roommates, Mia and Chloe, are going to help me bake, and you know how good they are in cookery class. They always get top marks for their cakes!"

Shannon's face fell a little as she glanced at Paige and Summer.

"I love a bit of competition, especially when I'm going to win," Abigail taunted. "In fact, I'm going to make a start right now." And she sauntered off, still smiling.

"Abigail's right," said Summer. "Mia and Chloe are brilliant at baking."

"I know, I know," Shannon groaned. "Me and my big mouth! Well, if we're going to beat the Peacock stall, we'd better get on with it." She sighed. "It would be brilliant to beat Abigail and shut her up, especially as the jumble sale is the last thing we'll ever do at Charm Hall before I have to go to great-aunt Agnes."

"Don't worry, I bet we find loads of good stuff," Summer said consolingly.

"And maybe we'll find out some interesting things about the history of Charm Hall School too," Paige suggested.

The cellars, which were near the school kitchens, were huge and ran the length of the whole house. As the girls climbed carefully down the steep stairs, they gasped at the vast space spread out below them. It was stuffed with boxes, trunks, baskets and bags.

"A lot of these boxes are just full of old textbooks and school stuff," Shannon said disappointedly, peering into them. Paige was poking around in the corner. "These are all full of old newspapers," she announced.

"Great-aunt Agnes's house is full of junk," Shannon said miserably. "She never throws anything out in case it comes in useful."

Paige glanced anxiously at her friend. She really hoped they could find some treasures to sell on their stall to cheer Shannon up a bit.

"Let's go in a bit further," Summer suggested.

The girls ventured deeper into the dark cellars.

"Ah, this looks a lot more interesting!" Shannon said with satisfaction as they reached a cellar where tables, chairs, bureaus and other pieces of furniture were piled higgledy-piggledy on top of each other, surrounded by boxes bulging with bric-a-brac.

"This must be the stuff from the house that Miss Linnet mentioned," said Summer. The headmistress

100

had explained that a lot of Lavinia Charm's furniture and ornaments had been stored in the cellars and that, as it all belonged to the school now, the girls could take whatever they liked for their stall.

The girls split up to explore the boxes. Paige peered into the one nearest to her and found some glass vases, most of which were chipped. Paige took out a couple that weren't too badly damaged. *They might sell*, she thought. She found an empty box and put the vases inside. She added a pretty but cracked china cup and saucer, a pair of binoculars with broken lenses, a grubby white tablecloth of delicate lace and a solitaire game with half the marbles missing.

"I've found this," Summer said, passing Paige an ornate gilt-framed mirror, shaped like a five-pointed star. Some of the silver background of the mirror had worn away in places and there was a fine crack down the middle. "What do you think of it?"

"It's a bit tatty but it's a nice shape," Paige said, adding it to the box. "Someone might buy it."

Shannon was also busy filling a box. Paige peeped inside to see what she'd found. There was a tiny marble clock which wasn't ticking, a blue glass perfume bottle with a chipped stopper and a cracked walking stick, its head shaped like a Chinese dragon.

"Hey, look at this," Shannon said, holding up a snowglobe with a tiny house inside that looked very much like Charm Hall.

Summer took it eagerly and gave it a shake, but the artificial snow had stuck together in lumps.

"Maybe I can fix it," Shannon said, but she didn't sound too hopeful. "I found this too," she added, holding up a small silver photo frame. Inside was a black and white photo of a smiling Lavinia Charm. She was seated at a piano, and on top of it was the black cat from the portrait who looked so much like Velvet.

"She looks nice, doesn't she?" Summer said. "I bet she wouldn't be very pleased that her great-grandson wants to close the school down."

The girls carried on searching and filling their boxes, working their way into every corner of the cellar.

Just as they were about to leave, Summer nudged Paige. "What's that book over there?" she asked curiously.

Paige saw a battered leather-bound book lying on a heap of moth-eaten curtains. She picked it up and leafed through it. "I think it's some sort of old journal or diary," she told Summer. "But the writing's really faded and difficult to read."

"Oh, well, somebody might buy it," Shannon said, so Paige placed the book in her box.

The three girls hurried back upstairs, carrying their tatty treasures. As they walked past the cookery room, they saw Abigail flicking through a pile of recipe books, noting down things to make for the bake stall. She looked up as she heard the girls approach and her eyes narrowed as she noticed the boxes in their arms.

"What have you got there?" she asked nosily, hurrying over. She glanced quickly into each box and then burst out laughing. "You're not going to try and sell *that* old rubbish, are you?" she chuckled. "Oh, well, it looks like our bake stall is going to win easily. No contest!" And she went back to the recipe books, still laughing.

Chapter Twelve

Paige sat cross-legged on her bed, holding a dusty old bottle. She'd picked it up in the cellar, thinking it might make a good candle holder. *It isn't particularly pretty though*, Paige thought with a sigh.

She, Summer and Shannon had spread their treasures out all over the floor ready for sorting. They had a bit of time before lights out to start cleaning up their stock for the stall, so the other two girls had gone to find some cleaning materials. Paige glanced around at the other items and had to admit that Abigail was right: the things they'd found didn't look very impressive. Would anyone want to buy them?

Paige's brow furrowed anxiously. It had become really important to Shannon that their stall did well, not only because she wanted to beat Abigail but because she wanted to leave Charm Hall on a high before she had to move in with the dreaded great-aunt Agnes. Paige didn't blame Shannon one bit – great-aunt Agnes sounded like a nightmare.

Determined to do her best to help Shannon, Paige took a tissue from the box on her bedside table and began rubbing at the dusty bottle. But the glass was cloudy and smeared and difficult to clean.

Miaow!

Paige jumped as Velvet leaped on to the bed. She hadn't even realized that the kitten was in the room.

"Velvet, you startled me!" Paige exclaimed, laughing.

Curious, the kitten padded over the duvet towards her. She sniffed the dusty bottle in Paige's hand, and immediately began to swish her tail from side to side.

Paige's eyes widened and she felt a thrill of excitement run through her as Velvet's whiskers quivered with that faint but unmistakable golden shimmer. Then, purring, Velvet sat down and began to wash her paw. The golden light had faded quickly, and Paige wondered for a second if she'd imagined it, but when she began rubbing at the bottle again, she couldn't believe her eyes. She was sure the bottle had been empty before, but now there was definitely something inside.

Paige redoubled her efforts to clean the glass. It was starting to gleam now, and she could see that inside the bottle there was a tiny ship. It had miniature round portholes, a wooden deck and white silk sails hanging from rigging made of golden thread. There was also a tiny ship's cat, a black one like Velvet, sitting on the deck.

"Oh!" Paige exclaimed. "That's fantastic!"

She held the bottle up to the light so that she could see inside more clearly. As she stared at the perfect tiny ship with its billowing white sails, the door opened.

"Here we are! And we're armed with lots of heavy-duty cleaning stuff," Summer said cheerily, coming in with Shannon behind her. "The cleaners were really nice and lent us loads of things."

"Are you all right, Paige?" asked Shannon. "Why are you smiling like that?"

"Remember that dusty old bottle from the cellar?" Paige asked in a dazed voice. "Well, here it is." And she held it up.

Summer and Shannon stared.

"It's cleaned up beautifully!" said Summer

admiringly. "But it was empty, wasn't it? How did you get that ship inside it?"

"I didn't." Paige shook her head. "Velvet did!" She described exactly what had happened.

"Look," Shannon said, pointing at Velvet, who was nosing around the dusty old snowglobe that stood on Paige's desk. "I wonder if Velvet can do something about that?"

The girls gathered together in the middle of the room and watched with excitement as Velvet gently sniffed the snowglobe. Then her tail began to twitch.

"Her whiskers are glowing again!" Shannon cried. "Look, Summer, they're all golden. And you can't say *that's* the sunlight because there isn't any – it's dark outside!"

"I know, I know," Summer murmured, her eyes fixed on the kitten. "This really *is* magic!"

She's convinced at last, Paige thought happily. Then she felt her heart begin to race as she noticed that the golden glow around Velvet's whiskers was growing bigger, spreading out around the kitten and enveloping her with dazzling light, like a halo.

"Look!" Paige cried. "I've never seen that before!"

"Wow!" Shannon whispered in awe as tiny

golden lights began to spin away from Velvet into every corner of the room. "This is amazing!"

Paige caught her breath as the lights began to slowly circle around them. A few seconds later they were whizzing round and round at fantastic speed, becoming a golden whirlwind that surrounded the girls as they stood dumbstruck in the middle of the room.

"What's happening?" Summer gasped in a dazed voice.

"Velvet's up to something!" Paige laughed, her gaze fixed on the swirling, whirling dazzle of lights that spun wildly around them.

The lights whizzed faster and faster, becoming a single continuous blur of gold.

"Look!" Paige shouted as the magical wind whistled around her ears. "Look at all the things we collected!"

The wind had swept up the snowglobe, the mirror, the binoculars and all the other dirty and broken items the girls had found in the cellars. As they stood rooted to the spot, the wind whipped the objects up into the air and they all began to fly around the room above the girls' heads, bathed in pure golden light.

Suddenly, as quickly as it had begun, the wind died away and Paige watched as all the objects, including the snowglobe, floated gently down and into their original positions.

A moment later the magical golden glow faded too. Immediately, Velvet jumped down from the desk on to the floor and sat staring enquiringly up at the girls.

"Velvet, what have you been up to?" Shannon gasped, grabbing the snowglobe which was clean and gleaming now. She shook it vigorously. As the girls watched, the snowflakes flew and whirled around the tiny house inside the globe.

"It works!" Shannon exclaimed, giving it another shake. Then she laughed in disbelief. "Look at this. It's spring now!"

Instead of snowflakes, pink cherry-blossom petals were now swirling around inside the globe.

"That's *real* magic!" Summer exclaimed, her eyes wide with amazement.

"Shake it again!" Paige suggested eagerly.

This time tiny bluebirds appeared, and all three girls gasped with delight.

"That's summer," Paige pointed out with a grin.

One more shake, and autumn leaves of red, orange and gold fluttered around inside the glass. The girls were delighted.

"It's autumn!" Summer said, looking quite dazed.

"It's Velvet's magic!" Shannon told her firmly, and Summer laughed and nodded.

"Thanks, Velvet!" Paige said gratefully, watching Shannon place the snowglobe carefully back on the desk. "You're such a clever kitten."

"What about the other things?" Shannon asked eagerly.

Paige picked up the binoculars and looked through them curiously. "The lenses aren't cracked any more," she announced. Then she ran over to the window and looked through the binoculars up into the night sky. "Oh, I can see a shooting star!" she exclaimed, her voice full of awe. "Ooh, and the moon's really clear. I can see right into the craters!"

Shannon and Summer crowded round her.

"What else?" asked Summer breathlessly.

"You two have a go," Paige said, handing the binoculars to Summer.

Summer took a look. "I can see a planet with

rings round it," she said. "The colours are amazing. Everything's so clear!"

"Which planet is it?" asked Paige.

"I think it might be Saturn," Summer replied. "I've seen it before through my dad's telescope, but these are much more powerful!" She took one last look and then handed the binoculars to Shannon.

Velvet was sitting on the rug watching the girls intently. Paige thought she looked very pleased with herself.

"Look!" Summer pointed out to the others. "The vases aren't chipped now, the holes in the tablecloth have vanished and the china cup isn't cracked any more!"

Paige grinned as she looked around at their collection of sparkling treasures. "Thanks to Velvet, our stall's going to be *brilliant*!" she cried.

Chapter Thirteen

The three girls smiled at Velvet who was now chasing a green marble from the solitaire game around the room.

"If only Velvet could talk," Summer said wistfully. "We still don't know where she came from and why she's got magic powers!"

Miaow, said Velvet obligingly, losing interest in the marble and going to explore under Summer's bed.

Paige picked up the marble and replaced it in the game. As she did, she noticed that none of the marbles were missing any more. "Look at this," she said, showing the game to Shannon and Summer. "Velvet's fixed this too!"

"Velvet, you're a star!" Shannon announced. "Everything's just perfect now!"

Suddenly Paige noticed the journal, the perfume bottle and the star-shaped mirror on Summer's bedside table.

"Not quite," she said. "Look! These are still the same." Paige picked up the three objects and handed them to Shannon and Summer. "How strange! They haven't changed a bit from when we found them in the cellars!"

"There must be a reason why Velvet's magic hasn't changed them," Summer said thoughtfully. "I wonder what it is."

"Never mind," said Shannon happily. "Thanks to Velvet, we're going to have a fantastic stall full of beautiful things that will make loads of money for charity. And I can't *wait* to see Abigail's face!"

"Come on then, you two," Paige said, giving Summer and Shannon a box each. "Let's clean these things up and pack them, ready for the fête."

* * *

"Doesn't the stall look *great*?" Shannon demanded as she stepped back to look at the bric-a-brac which filled three long tables. "Is that everything, Paige?"

Paige nodded, pushing the last of the empty boxes under the stall. "Yep, that's it." She joined Shannon to survey their stall from the front. Thanks to Velvet's magic and their own hard work, all their treasures looked beautiful, Paige thought happily. Well, except for the journal, the perfume bottle and the mirror, but they were half hidden out of sight, at the back.

It was a Saturday and the day of the Founder's Day fête. Yesterday, the girls had been told that Charm Hall School would be closing in just over a week's time. When they'd heard the news, Paige had realized that they'd all been hoping for some sort of miracle that would save the school, but now it was clear that that wasn't going to happen. Everyone in the school had seemed subdued and depressed all through Friday evening, but this morning all the girls were putting a brave face on things for the fête. Everyone wanted it to go well.

Luckily, the day had dawned bright and sunny. As Paige looked around the playing field, she could see teachers and girls rushing around amongst the stalls, bouncy castle and other attractions, putting the finishing touches to everything before the gates opened for the visitors.

"Everyone's worked really hard," remarked Shannon, moving the snowglobe to a more prominent position. "I just hope we make lots of money for charity."

Summer arrived just then, carrying a cash box. "Mrs Bloomfield's given me loads of change, so we're all set!" she said, placing the box on the table. "Have you seen Abigail's stall? It *does* look good."

Paige and Shannon looked across to the bake stall. It was crammed with home-made cakes, sweets, buns and biscuits, and they all looked delicious.

"Oh, well, may the best stall win!" Shannon said with a grin.

"Don't look now," Paige whispered, "but here comes Abigail herself."

Abigail was hurrying across the field, carrying an enormous iced fruit cake which was clearly the centrepiece of the bake stall. Her inquisitive eyes scanned the girls' stall as she passed by, and Paige saw her face drop as she noted all the beautiful treasures on the tables.

"Is something wrong, Abigail?" Shannon asked innocently.

Abigail didn't reply. She just stuck her nose in the air and hurried off. The girls grinned.

"The gates are open!" Summer pointed out, as crowds of people began to flood on to the playing field.

"Good afternoon, everyone!" Miss Linnet announced. She was standing, microphone in hand, on the small stage that had been set up in the middle of the playing field. "The official opening of the Founder's Day fête is going to be carried out by one of our guests. Please welcome Mr Kennedy whose company has acted as solicitors for the school for the last hundred years!"

Everyone applauded as Mr Kennedy, an elderly, grey-haired man, stepped forward and took the microphone. "Good afternoon, everyone," he said. "As Miss Linnet explained, my family's company have looked after the school's affairs ever since it opened. We were asked to do so by Miss Lavinia Charm herself. She loved the school and would, I'm sure, be very sad to see it close. But today, let's focus on enjoying the fête and all the wonderful activities the girls and their teachers have worked so hard to provide. I declare this fête open!"

There was more applause and then everyone headed over to the stalls.

"Here they come!" Paige murmured.

From that moment on, the girls were rushed off their feet. Velvet's magic had made their finds so beautiful that people flocked to their stall.

"Paige, have you got any change?" Summer asked urgently. "Someone wants to buy the ship in a bottle."

Paige handed Summer a handful of silver. "I can't believe how well it's going," she whispered.

"Me neither," Summer agreed happily.

Shannon, who had just sold the marble clock, only had time to wink at them.

"Hello, girls." Joan, the dinner lady, had managed to make her way to the front of the crowd and now stood there beaming at them. "Have you seen that lovely kitten recently?"

"Hi, Joan," said Paige. "Yes, we saw Velvet this morning." She didn't mention that the kitten had been in their dorm room.

"I wonder what's going to happen to her when the school closes," Joan went on.

The three friends exchanged an anxious look. Joan had touched on their greatest worry of all: if Paige, Summer and Shannon weren't at Charm Hall any more, what would happen to Velvet?

"We don't know," Summer said sadly.

"Well, I could carry on feeding her," Joan suggested. "I don't live far away: just at the end of the school drive, near the village shop."

"That would be wonderful," Shannon said, and Paige smiled with relief, but deep down inside she knew that part of her was still hoping that none of them would have to leave and that the school wouldn't have to close at all. It was looking less and less likely though. Her flight to Dubai was already booked.

"You have some gorgeous things on your stall, girls," Joan went on. "Where did you find them all?"

"In the school cellars," Summer replied.

"And they're all very reasonably priced!" Shannon pointed out cheekily.

Joan laughed. "You're a great saleswoman, Shannon, but I've already got my eye on

119

something." She picked up the snowglobe and gave it a little shake so that the snowflakes began to whirl. "Isn't this pretty?"

"Shake it again," Paige suggested, smiling at Summer and Shannon.

Joan gasped with delight as the seasons inside the globe changed from winter to spring to summer to autumn. "Well, that's one of the loveliest things I've ever seen!" she exclaimed. "And the house inside looks a bit like Charm Hall, so it will remind me of the school after it's closed. You've got a sale, girls!"

"Great," Shannon said, wrapping the snowglobe carefully in tissue paper. "Another satisfied customer!"

By the end of the day, the girls' stall was almost bare. As the girls had suspected, the things which Velvet had ignored, the journal, the perfume bottle and the mirror, hadn't sold. The only other thing on the table was the photo of Lavinia Charm.

"Phew!" Shannon groaned. "That was exhausting!"

"But just look how much money we made!" Paige exclaimed.

"And, who knows, we might still sell these," Summer added, pointing at the leftovers.

"Girls, this is wonderful!" Miss Linnet exclaimed, coming over to the stall as everyone was packing up at the end of the fête. "You've sold almost everything."

Paige, Shannon and Summer grinned at each other as Miss Linnet smiled proudly at them. But just then, Paige was surprised to see Velvet appear out of nowhere at the headmistress's side. The kitten leaped up on to the table, knocking over the framed photo of Lavinia Charm as she did so. Miss Linnet laughed as Paige quickly picked the kitten up.

"Oh, Velvet, you're not for sale!" Paige whispered as she carefully put Velvet down on the grass.

"What's this?" Miss Linnet asked, picking up the fallen picture and looking closely at the photo of Lavinia. "You know," she said slowly, "I think I'll buy this for myself. It will remind me of all the wonderful times I've had at Charm Hall."

Shannon wrapped up the photo and handed it to Miss Linnet, who went on her way looking pleased with her purchase. The girls packed the last few items away and looked around for Velvet but the kitten had vanished again, as quickly as she had appeared.

It was exactly one week later and the girls were sitting sadly in their dorm room, playing with Velvet for what Paige thought might be her last time ever! It was heartbreaking to think about. Paige was flying to Dubai early the following morning and her belongings were already packed up and ready for her departure. Shannon and Summer would be leaving along with all the other pupils of Charm Hall School later in the day. Paige knew that Shannon was particularly miserable, although her friend was trying to put on a brave face. Great-aunt Agnes had already written to say that she would be meeting Shannon at the station.

"Even Velvet doesn't feel like playing," Summer noted, as the little kitten ignored the ribbon Paige was dangling in front of her and curled up to go to sleep.

Paige put the ribbon down with a sigh. "We've still got an hour before dinner," she said. "What shall we do?"

"We could go and say goodbye to Miss Linnet," Shannon suggested. "You're leaving so early, Paige, you probably won't get the chance tomorrow morning."

Paige nodded. It was a good idea. She didn't want to miss saying goodbye to her favourite teacher.

The girls headed downstairs together and knocked politely on the door of Miss Linnet's office.

"Come in," they heard Miss Linnet call from inside.

Shannon turned the handle and they all filed in. Miss Linnet was sitting at her desk with Mr Kennedy, the solicitor. Paige guessed they must be going over some of the legal details of the school's closure. The photo of Lavinia Charm that Miss Linnet had bought from the white elephant stall was now proudly displayed on her desk.

"Hello, girls," Miss Linnet said, smiling at them. "Are you all packed and ready, Paige? You've got an early start in the morning."

Paige nodded. "That's why we came," she said. "We didn't mean to interrupt . . ."

"But Paige wanted to say goodbye," Summer put in.

"We all did," Shannon added.

Miss Linnet smiled a little sadly and leaned across her desk towards the girls. "That's quite all right, girls. I'm very sorry to have to say goodbye to you at all," she began.

As she spoke, Paige suddenly found herself distracted by what she was sure was the flick of a tail — a *kitten's* tail. She turned to look, and to her amazement, there was Velvet, trotting happily across Miss Linnet's office!

Paige tried to gesture quietly to Summer and Shannon so that Miss Linnet wouldn't see, but it was too late. Velvet jumped up on to Mr Kennedy's lap with a very loud *Miaow!*

Miss Linnet gasped in surprise.

"Wherever did *you* come from?" Mr Kennedy said to the kitten, looking slightly shocked.

Good question, Paige thought. The door to the office was shut and so were all the windows. *Velvet must be using her magic again*, Paige decided. *But why?*

Mr Kennedy tried to pick Velvet up, but Velvet slipped easily through his fingers and raced across the room. She skittered merrily over to the

124

windows and disappeared beneath the hem of the long velvet curtains.

"I don't know how she got in," Shannon said, rushing after the kitten, "but we'll take her back outside right now."

"Yes, we'll get her, Miss Linnet!" Paige added hurriedly, thinking that Miss Linnet might start asking awkward questions about Velvet if they didn't get the kitten out of the room quickly. She dashed over to the window with Summer at her heels.

The three girls pulled the curtain aside, trying to find Velvet.

"There she is!" Mr Kennedy cried, and Paige saw Velvet dart out from underneath one of the curtains, just as the curtain itself somehow came free of the rail and collapsed on top of the girls.

"Help!" Paige gasped, as she was enveloped in swathes of velvet and everything went dark.

The girls managed to free themselves from the fabric, just in time to see Velvet dodge Miss Linnet's grasp and disappear under a cabinet on the far side of the room. Shannon raced over and lay down on the floor, reaching under the cabinet with one arm.

But, at that moment, Velvet shot out from under the cabinet, raced back across the room and leaped up on to the top of a cupboard and from there on to a bookshelf above. Paige and Summer collided with each other in their attempts to grab Velvet as she whizzed past. And Mr Kennedy tripped over a chair as he too lunged for the kitten.

"I'm stuck!" Shannon wailed, still lying on the floor. "I can't get my arm out!"

Miss Linnet rushed over to help. "This kitten has got us all on the run!" she remarked with a frown as she helped a red-faced Shannon to her feet.

Velvet, this is not *a good time for playing games!* Paige thought anxiously. Maybe Miss Linnet would call an animal charity to take Velvet away if the kitten proved too troublesome.

Her thoughts were interrupted by a cry of alarm from Summer. Paige looked up to see that Velvet was now trotting along the tops of the books on the shelf and they were shifting dangerously.

"Look out!" Summer cried and everyone jumped out of the way as the books began to topple off the shelf and crash to the floor.

Meanwhile Velvet seemed to be thoroughly

enjoying the havoc she was causing. She leaped down from the bookshelf, ran lightly between Mr Kennedy's legs and jumped up on to Miss Linnet's desk.

"Velvet's causing chaos!" Shannon murmured to Paige. "We *have* to get her out of here!"

Paige nodded. But how did you catch a magical kitten who so obviously didn't want to be caught?

"Come here, Velvet!" she called softly, making her way quietly over to Miss Linnet's desk as the others picked up the fallen books.

Velvet was sniffing curiously at the photograph of Lavinia Charm near the edge of the desk. She nuzzled it with her soft pink nose and the silver frame wobbled slightly.

"Uh-oh," Paige groaned, guessing what was about to happen.

She dashed over to grab the picture, but she was too late. Velvet batted it with one paw and the photograph tumbled to the floor. There was a loud *crack* as the glass broke into several pieces.

Velvet remained sitting on the desk, looking at Paige triumphantly. Anxiously Paige bent down to see if the photograph itself was damaged, as

Shannon finally managed to sweep Velvet up in her arms and carry her over to the window. Summer opened it and Velvet immediately bounded outside, her attention caught by a stray leaf dancing in the wind.

Mr Kennedy sat down in his chair again, with a sigh of relief.

"Don't touch the broken glass," Miss Linnet told Paige. "I'll get the caretaker to clean it up."

Carefully Paige picked up the picture frame, but then she saw that it wasn't just the glass which had broken. The frame itself had cracked and was coming apart. As Paige turned it over, she noticed a piece of yellowed paper tucked behind the picture.

"That's funny," she said, puzzled. "There's something hidden in the frame!"

Chapter Fourteen

"What is it?" Shannon asked eagerly.

"It's a piece of paper," said Paige, pulling it gently out of the frame. "And it's got some writing on it."

"Read it, Paige!" urged Summer.

Paige carefully unfolded the paper which was brittle and worn with age.

" 'This is an addendum to the final will and testament of Lavinia Charm of Charm Hall'," she read out slowly.

"Addendum!" Miss Linnet repeated, her face lighting up with joy. "Paige, let me see that!"

Paige handed the paper to Miss Linnet, while

Summer and Shannon stared at each other in excitement. Even Mr Kennedy couldn't resist peering over Miss Linnet's shoulder.

Miss Linnet looked up.

"Mr Kennedy?" she asked, her voice shaking.

The elderly solicitor took the paper from Miss Linnet for a closer look. The girls waited impatiently for him to read it fully.

"Well!" Mr Kennedy said at last, looking very surprised. "This document will have to be verified, of course. But it seems to be the addendum that everyone believed Lavinia Charm had made to her will. It leaves the house and grounds of Charm Hall to the school for ever!"

"Oh!" Paige exclaimed, her heart beginning to race. "Does this mean that the school won't have to close?" She felt a big smile spreading over her face as she glanced at Summer and Shannon. They looked as thrilled and excited as she was.

"Not if this document is genuine," Mr Kennedy declared thoughtfully. "And I have to say that it certainly looks like it is!"

Miss Linnet clapped her hands in delight and Paige felt a huge rush of relief as she threw her arms around Shannon and Summer. They hugged each other hard, laughing and jumping up and down with joy.

"Velvet's done it!" Summer whispered. "She's saved the school!"

"Charm Hall isn't closing after all!" laughed Shannon. "And now I won't have to stay with nasty great-aunt Agnes! Isn't it fantastic?"

"It's brilliant!" Paige declared, her eyes shining. She was so happy, she felt as if she was going to burst. Now she wouldn't have to start at a new school hundreds of miles away in Dubai. *This is one of the best days of my whole life – and it's all thanks to Velvet!* she thought.

"Attention, girls!" Miss Linnet rose from her seat at the head of the teachers' table and surveyed the dining hall, a happy smile on her face.

It was the end of the evening meal, and the girls had just finished a delicious dinner which had been prepared as a special last meal before the school closed, but which had turned into a celebratory feast instead. Paige, Shannon and Summer had spent the last half-hour before dinner unpacking and phoning their parents to tell them the news. Paige's mum had promised to move her flight to the end of term so that Paige could join her family in Dubai for the summer holidays, but she would be back in the autumn, along with Shannon and Summer.

Everyone was in high spirits, and the dining hall was filled with excited chatter and laughter.

"Well, what can I say?" the headteacher went on. "Never in my wildest dreams did I think that we would be able to keep the school open! But now we have the precious addendum, and we owe it all to the three girls who found that photograph . . ." She pointed at Paige, Shannon and Summer. "Stand up and take a bow, girls."

Blushing, Paige and the others got to their feet to a huge round of applause which almost lifted the roof off the dining hall.

"I wish Velvet could be here too," Paige whispered, under cover of the noise. "This is really all down to her."

Summer and Shannon nodded in agreement.

"And just to round things off nicely, I'm happy to announce that the white elephant stall raised the most money of all at our fête!" Miss Linnet laughed. "So once again, well done, girls, and well done, Hummingbird House!"

Paige, Shannon and Summer couldn't resist glancing at Abigail. She looked a bit annoyed, but she was bravely clapping along with everyone else.

"You know what?" Shannon said as they hurried back to the dorm after dinner. "I think Abigail was so glad the school isn't closing, she didn't really mind that we made the most money!"

Summer and Paige laughed and nodded.

"At least Velvet can share our celebration," Paige added. She had a paper napkin filled with salmon sandwiches in her pocket.

Velvet was lying on the window sill, waiting for them. She gave a pleased little chirrup when they opened the door and bounded over to Paige, staring up at her expectantly.

"She knows I've got something tasty," Paige laughed. She spread the napkin on the floor, and scraped the salmon out of the sandwiches for Velvet. The kitten gobbled it up greedily.

"So now we're all going to stay at Charm Hall," Shannon said with satisfaction. "And Velvet too."

"She turned up at just the right moment, didn't she?" Summer pointed out. "I wonder what else she's got in store for us!"

Paige grinned as she watched the kitten delicately cleaning her paws with her tiny pink tongue. "I just *know* we're going to have lots more magical adventures with Velvet the witch cat!" she sighed happily.

And Velvet blinked her golden eyes as if she completely agreed.

If you want to read more
about the **magic** at
Charm Hall, then
turn over for the start of
the neXt adventure ...

Chapter One

"Good morning, girls!"

"Good morning, Miss Collins," Paige Hart replied, along with everybody else in the room. It was a hot day, and her form group were about to start their English class. A bumblebee was droning outside the open classroom window, and Paige could hear the *thwack* of tennis balls coming from the courts. Paige blew a stray red curl out of her eyes and fanned herself with her exercise book. Summertime had definitely arrived at Charm Hall boarding school, that was for sure!

Miss Collins turned to chalk something up on

the blackboard, and Paige smiled as she saw her friend Shannon Carroll crane her neck to see what the teacher was writing. That was Shannon all over: she hated being kept in suspense. Paige's gaze drifted over to Summer, who was staring into space in a world of her own. Her two best friends were like chalk and cheese but Paige wouldn't have had it any other way.

She had only been at Charm Hall a short while, but it already felt like home. So much had happened since she'd said goodbye to her parents several weeks ago! *Let's see*, Paige thought to herself. *Since Mum and Dad moved to Dubai with Dad's new job, I've started a new school, made two brilliant new friends, and met a mischievous kitten, Velvet, who just happens to be magical!*

"I have a special announcement to make this morning," Miss Collins declared, turning to face the class.

Paige switched her attention back to her teacher to see that Miss Collins had written *A Midsummer Night's Dream* on the blackboard. Paige's class had been studying the Shakespeare play since the beginning of term. Paige wondered what Miss Collins was about to tell them.

"As you are the youngest students at Charm Hall, you may not know that it is a tradition at our school for one year group to put on a summer play at the end of term," Miss Collins said. "It's quite a big occasion, with the whole school invited to watch, and parents, too, of course. And I'm pleased to tell you that this year, the Year Fives have been chosen to act, direct and produce the play." She smiled and pointed at the blackboard. "And yes, you're going to be putting on *A Midsummer Night's Dream!*"

"Cool!" exclaimed Shannon, with a big smile at Paige and Summer.

Paige felt a rush of excitement. "This is going to be fun!" she whispered, and Summer grinned.

Everyone in the class was talking excitedly about the news. Paige really liked the play, with the fairy king and queen, and Puck the mischievous fairy. And she loved all the funny bits, like when Bottom the weaver got the head of a donkey!

The class hushed as Miss Collins began talking again. "I'll be holding auditions for parts in the play at the beginning of next week," she told them. "But, as well as actors, I'll need students to work behind the scenes too: making costumes, painting scenery, operating the lights and sound effects . . . all sorts of things. I'll also need an assistant director and a stage manager."

Abigail Carter's hand shot up. "Please, miss, what will they do? The stage manager and assistant director, I mean."

Miss Collins smiled at the keen look on Abigail's face. "The assistant director will be working with me, to guide the actors through their performances," she replied. "And the stage manager will be responsible for organizing all the behind-the-scenes activities. Things like overseeing the props and sets, and running the backstage and onstage areas during the show."

Shannon was looking particularly interested, Paige noticed. She smiled. Out of the three friends, Shannon was definitely the bossiest, in the nicest possible way, of course! Paige could tell that the idea of organizing a whole play really appealed to Shannon.

"If anybody is interested in any of the behind-the-scenes roles, do come and speak to me directly," Miss Collins went on. She smiled around the classroom, her eyes shining. "There will be something for everyone to do, and we're all going to have great fun!" she said. "But before anything else, we'd better finish reading the play, so if you all turn to Act Four, Scene One, we'll find out what happens next."

Paige flicked through the pages of the play, a big smile on her face. She loved painting and drawing, and she was already thinking about doing something creative for the play. Scenery painting sounded good. She was looking forward to talking to Summer and Shannon about it at lunchtime.

After their English class, Paige and her friends headed for the dining hall to get lunch.

"Putting on the play is going to be great," Shannon said happily. "Which parts are you two thinking of trying out for?"

Before either Paige or Summer could reply, Abigail Carter barged past them. "Of course, I'll get the assistant director role," she was boasting loudly to her friend Mia. "Miss Collins gave me a really high mark for my last essay on the play, and even said that I clearly understood the workings of

A Midsummer Night's Dream really well," she said, sounding very confident. "It's obvious I'll get to direct. And with your background, Mia, you're bound to get the role of Queen Titania!"

Paige and her friends joined the queue for food behind Abigail and Mia, and Shannon rolled her eyes at Abigail's comments.

"What does Abigail mean, 'with Mia's background'?" Paige asked curiously, keeping her voice low.

"Mia's mum is a famous actress," Summer explained in a whisper. "Diana West."

"Yeah. I reckon that's why Abigail doesn't boss Mia around as much as she does everyone else," Shannon added quietly. "She probably loves the idea of being friends with Diana West's daughter."

The three friends collected their food and sat down to eat.

"Forget Abigail and Mia, anyway," Paige said. "What are you two going to try out for? I'd quite like to help out with the set design, especially if I can paint the backdrops."

Shannon twirled some spaghetti around her fork. "I'd love to be assistant director," she admitted, and then her eyes flicked over to the next table, where Abigail was still talking about herself in a loud voice. "Although Miss Carter over there seems to think she already has *that* job in the bag."

"Don't be so sure," Summer said. "Miss Collins is good at seeing straight through Abigail's sucking up."

"And you'd make a great assistant director," Paige added. "You're brilliant at bossing people around — and as your roommates, we should know, right, Summer?"

Shannon pretended to look shocked and then laughed, but Summer was staring into space.

"Summer?" Paige repeated. Her friend seemed very thoughtful all of a sudden. "What are you thinking about?"

Summer bit her lip. "The thing is, I'd love to be Puck," she confessed, "but . . ."

"But nothing!" Shannon told her. "You'd make a fabulous Puck!"

Summer shrugged. "I'm worried I'll get stage fright," she said. "I don't know if I even dare audition."

"You should go for it," Paige told her encouragingly. "I think you'd be fantastic."

Summer's cheeks had turned pink. "Thanks," she said shyly, "but I'm not sure. Don't tell anyone I'm thinking about trying out for Puck, will you?" she added hastily.

"Don't worry," Paige reassured her friend. "You should know by now we're all experts at keeping secrets." She forked some tuna from her salad into a napkin, so that she could sneak it upstairs as a treat for Velvet. Then she grinned and added quietly, "Especially *kitten*-sized secrets!"

With magic in the air at Charm Hall, this is one boarding school where anything can happen!

A mysterious diary reveals to Paige, Summer and Shannon that a precious sapphire is hidden in the school grounds.

Then they discover someone is trying to steal the jewel! Can the girls – with Velvet's help - stop them in time

Hodder Children's Books

A division of Hachette Children's Books

With magic in the air at Charm Hall, this is one boarding school where anything can happen!

It's Christmas time and the choir enter a carol competition. But then they find out another school is singing the same carols!

Velvet takes Paige, Summer and Shannon back in time to solve the mystery of why the famous Mona Lisa is smiling and they find a way to save the choir, too.

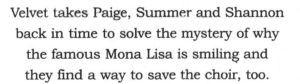

Hodder Children's Books

A division of Hachette Children's Books